READING BETWEEN THE LINES

Anna Newman

and

John Cliff

With cover illustrated by Olga Tramontin

Best Wishes
John Cliff

Edited by Geoffrey Thatcher

Anna Newman

ISBN 978-0-9929577-3-5

Published by Chadgreen Publishing Limited, Telford

Printed and bound in Great Britain by
Think Ink Limited, Ipswich, Suffolk

For Joan – our inspiration

Contents

ERRATUM

Page 49 Line 11

As any steam railway buff knows, the designer of this locomotive was Ivatt, not Stanier as stated. Number 43106, lovingly called the Flying Pig, is restored and running on the Severn Valley Railway

John Cliff
2014

The Bay
by John Cliff

The air clung to an eddy of grey mist as I lumbered across the water meadow, creel and rod bag swinging from my shoulder, head down to keep my eyes on the narrow footpath - or was it a cattle track? Fortunately I had not forgotten my way to the river and to a favourite autumn haunt, where the glides deepen then turn into a different kind of eddy: a dark watery swirl under the alder trees, soon dissipating against a protrusion of flood eroded bank. We always knew it as The Bay. An almost deafening silence encompassed me as I trudged towards the stile that would soon loom from the greyness. The next field, saturated with a heavy dew, was creaking in swampy oases, where the silence was interrupted by a moorhen awakening to the call of All Saints Day, heralded, strangely, by eight ghostly chimes of the distant church clock My gumboots squelched in the soft earth, alarming a rook scavenging for breakfast. Suddenly there was an eruption of indignation as the disturbed bird joined its company, unseen but heard in a chain reaction of cawing and clattering hastily diminishing into the ether. I looked up, seeing only the heavens in monotone punctuated by a weak sun. Firmer ground of the river bank was reached and my old fishing spot, strangely familiar, a grassy ledge below waiting for its long absent tenant.

No hurry as I surveyed the widening landscape, the early sun replacing the grey shroud with a dressing of silver over the fields. A herd of cows strolled ever so slowly from a farmyard a quarter of a mile away, their breaths steaming as rhythmically as their pace. The sky opened to a hazy blue, the air feeling a degree warmer. I took up residence on the ledge and set out my stall. Minutes later I cast out my first line and manoeuvred it to avoid a collection of fallen leaves on the surface, the float sitting comfortably on the edge of the current, myself comfortably on the creel, back against the bank.

What better way to engage with nature, observing life in and out of the water. A coot came close to where I sat, pecking the margins, then a robin arrived to inspect my bait tin, deciding to stay awhile. Near the opposite bank there was a commotion as two mallards vied for space on landing in a reed bed followed by some small fish leaping from the water as if escaping from a predator lurking beneath.

Fingers of mist chased the meandering river's course, refusing to submit to the sun's warmth. I heard the church clock strike nine. An hour, yet no time at all had passed. My float was picked up by the current and carried out into the glide. It dipped but I was too embroiled in the surroundings to respond in time. I replaced the bait and cast out again. The robin returned to sweep up crumbs as I opened a flask of hot coffee and in doing so I alarmed a vole swimming towards my bank. The creature dived and continued its journey underwater before scrambling into a tangle of exposed roots.

The Bay was at the end of a row of alder trees which hugged the bank along much of the river, providing food and shelter for birds, insects and mammals. Downstream, the eroded bank supported patches of hawthorn and scrub, also access where cattle would gather for refreshment in the shallows. Today was not for wallowing in an icy river, their thirst better quenched in the wet meadows. A few cows ambled along the path above me to inspect this human sitting by the water. They snorted disapprovingly, stared as only cows can, then retreated to ruminate with more interesting company.

I used to fish here in high summer but it is, to me, an autumn venue. All my best roach came from this swim late in the year, sometimes a perch from the quiet pool at the end where summer's embers reflect yellow and gold in the water. I take my lunchbox from the creel: strange to use that description nowadays. A creel is an old term, and mine is old, made from willow: recommended to be soaked in water from time to time to keep it supple. I'm afraid it rarely receives such purposeful treatment, but then it gets wet in the rain. No rain today, no time today. The church clock strikes the half hour. Half past what I don't know. The trees across from where I sit respond to a slight breeze and set free all but the last vestige of spent leaves, a few settling on the current like tiny craft. Perhaps it's because the air feels colder and a new mist creeps down the river. The sun appears to be waning far too early, even for late autumn, its gleam gone from the pool. My float sits patiently in the eddy, collecting leaves. The cows have disappeared. Only the robin stands guard over my lunchbox, now depleted of its contents apart from a scattering of crumbs.

Too soon the light dwindles as the mist returns with a vengeance. Fishless, I dismantle the gear and pack it away. Redbreast takes over the tenancy with gusto. I take a last look at the old haunt and return a different way, upstream along the river bank towards the church. Occasionally the afternoon sun pierces the murkiness, the church spire standing in illuminated splendour for brief moments. On reaching a gap in the lichen encrusted stone wall I squeeze through into the churchyard. Lime trees are showering the day's mist over me as I leave the river towards the lych-gate. Nearby I ponder over a once familiar headstone, weathered over the years, its inscription still legible.

We used to go fishing together, all the way down to The Bay. But that was forty-five autumns ago. It's taken that long. Seems like no time at all.

Whiteout

by Anna Newman

Now snow is a wonderful thing if you're a child, or you're sitting in front of a warm fire looking out on a Christmas-card world. But not if you're middle-aged, unfit, and lost on a mountain. Well I say mountain; my friend, Rory, in the pub said it is just a very large hill.

'Only 2000 feet,' he grinned. 'And that's 1999 feet more than you can climb.'

Everyone laughed and I coloured up. My pride was hurt.

'That's all you know,' I retorted. 'I might just climb it one day.'

Rory nearly choked on his beer. 'Hundred quid says you won't make it.' He was that confident.

Now it happened my electricity bill had dropped on my doormat that morning – for £98. I stood up and held out my hand.

'Hundred quid says I will,' I announced. Brave words.

I started out just before lunchtime, mobile phone, sandwiches and flask in my rucksack. The weather was stormy, with a keen north wind and scudding grey clouds, but I wasn't unduly worried. I was quite warm in my old parka, tracksuit bottoms and ancient trainers. In my rucksack, snuggling next to my lunch, was my camera and the torn off front page of The Sun newspaper, chosen on account of the huge headlines. My plan was to set the camera on delayed action at the top and pop in front of it, holding the page before me to prove that I had made it, with the view behind me. I had told no-one of my adventure; it was to be a surprise in the pub that evening – more of a shock to Rory, who would have to hand over the money, red faced I hoped.

2000 feet should only take a couple of hours, I thought; I'd be back for a hot bath by teatime.

It all started well. I walked the lower slopes steadily, following the pathway as it meandered between clumps of trees thick with ivy. Then the terrain gradually became steeper and my progress slowed. I met one or two fellow walkers and waved a greeting but they were descending. After a while I began to feel very alone. The leafless beeches and oaks gave way to tall pines, and the pathway narrowed into gloomy corridors.

I stopped then and sank down onto a fallen log to rest my legs. My calves were protesting mightily and I rubbed them. My lunch was soon eaten. The wind had grown stronger in the last half hour, blowing darker clouds over the pine trees.

When I hauled my rucksack on again, I felt the first drops of rain sting my face. For a moment I hesitated. The lower slopes were just behind me and the gradient before me seemed formidable. But I talked sternly to myself and struck out upwards.

My determination carried me several hundred yards up rough scree. Sometimes I had to go on hands and feet to keep my grip. Sometimes my feet slid back more than they gained ground. The wind had now gathered strength, menacing and whining in the trees. And the rain now fell steadily, turning the pathway into slippery mud.

My breath came in small sobs as I persevered along the track. I reckoned I must be more than halfway up by now. It would be stupid to turn around. I briefly imagined the hated electricity bill and set myself resolutely towards the top.

I concentrated hard on every step. My world had focussed down into the view in front of my face, that of mud, small stones and tangled roots, with rivulets of rain dashing downwards, soaking my trainers. Then came the snow, huge flakes whipped by an icy wind which cut my face and hands.

Blinded by the sudden blizzard I slipped and skidded down several feet on my front, cutting my nose and chin on the stony soil that was almost hidden beneath a covering of snow. My blood dripped onto the white flakes and I cried. When I hauled myself up again and leaned against a fir tree for support, I was horrified to realise how dark it was and how thoroughly the snow was filling in all the spaces between the trees. The blizzard blew mercilessly and horizontally.

When I came to a swift flowing stream I crossed it clumsily, losing my balance on the freezing stones and plunging my feet into the biting waters. Somehow I scrambled up the far bank and lay on the snow-covered ground, tears of frustration mingling with the flakes.

Very soon afterwards I lost the trail. I could see no way forward. Time was getting on and darkness had set in. I was by now in a state of terror. Snow lay all around me: I was on some kind of plateau but the sky and the ground were now indistinguishable from each other. I couldn't even see the way I'd come. The snow had covered my footsteps with scary efficiency. I stood unsteadily, quite alone in the world, with the wind in a frenzy about my body. Would I freeze to death I wondered? With teeth chattering uncontrollably I edged forward in the snow, soggy trainers submerged at each step. It was then, with the horror of my predicament that I swung my rucksack off my back and forced my frozen fingers to fish out my mobile phone – pride could go to hell.

I stabbed furiously at the buttons. I had to get help. Then in my trembling state my phone slipped from my grasp into the snow.

I swore and dropped to my knees, fumbling blindly in the soft wetness. I was now truly scared and crawled forward, sobbing bitterly. Finally I forced myself to my feet. I had lost the phone, probably had crawled over it. I turned to search again and it was then the howling wind blew me off balance. I staggered back helplessly and fell. My left leg suddenly slipped into nothingness. In the primitive panic of survival I grabbed at the air and caught a branch, rough and icy, between my hands. My right leg caught in a hooked root. I was stuck. I had no strength to pull myself up and no strength to hold on. I was going to die.

Some moments later I thought I heard a voice, but I could hardly discern it from the gale that raged about me. Then I saw a faint light…just above me.

'Hello there,' the voice shouted. I tried to call out but could only manage a helpless gasp.

'Don't move,' came another shout. The light dazzled my eyes as I looked up. I could just make out the shape of a tall figure holding some sort of lantern. He wedged the light into a tree, angling it so the light fell on my face and arms.

'Oh thank God,' I gasped.

'Don't talk,' he ordered. 'Now, give me your hand.'

Inch by painful inch he helped me edge my way up to safety. Sometimes he lost his footing on the rock beneath the snow and we had to pause, trying to get our breath in the stinging gale. Finally I collapsed onto the snow at his feet. He gripped me in his strong hands and pulled me away from the drop.

'You nearly went into the quarry,' he said. As he held the light I looked at him through the blizzard. He was tall and angular, with a shapeless woollen coat tied roughly round his middle. His trousers were tucked into wellington boots. His face was more difficult to make out – he had a long beard, icy in the fierce wind, bushy unkempt eyebrows and deepset eyes. But his voice was kind and he had a gentle manner, at odds with his obvious strength.

'What are you doing up here alone, lady?' he asked. He had to shout to be heard over the wind.

'Had a bet to climb the mountain,' I explained. 'Stupid...'

He nodded gravely at me, holding me firmly against the wind.

'What are you doing here, come to that,' I asked.

'I need help for my dog,' he shouted. 'Her name is Bess.'

Before I could reply, he pulled me round and pushed me before him. 'Come lady,' he said. 'You'll die out here in the cold. I have a hut nearby, you can take shelter there.

All my instincts of self-preservation screamed in my head but what choice did I have? He could be a killer but so could the snow. He led the way with a sureness that amazed me. It all looked the same to me, just snow and darkness. Sometimes he pulled me ahead, sometimes he appeared behind me to help me up a slope. Finally, with the last shreds of my strength evaporating, he stopped before a latched door of an old hut that was almost obliterated by a snowdrift.

He held the lantern high. 'Go in lady,' he ordered. 'Be careful for it is dark. There's a table in the middle of the hut. On it you'll find candle and matches. Once you light that you'll find all you need.'

My frozen fingers fumbled with the latch. The wind whipped round us and his light grew fainter. 'Where are you going?' I said. 'Why aren't you...?'

'I will join you soon, he said.

'I don't know how to thank you,' I said, as the door crashed open.

You can help my dog,' he said in a grave voice.

'I'm not a vet,' I shouted over the wind. 'What's wrong with her?'

But he had turned away and was lost in the night.

'Don't go,' I begged, but I was talking to the blizzard.

I groped in the velvet blackness of the hut, after shutting the door behind me, not without a struggle. The table found my shins before I found it. I groped for the candle and matches. They were there, just as the man said. I felt a huge surge of relief as the hut seemed to come to life with the light. It was then that I remembered the dog. 'Good dog,' I called out tentatively. 'Good dog.'

I heard the reassuring thump of a tail against the wooden floor from the back of the hut, lost in the shadows.

The hut was quite simply furnished. A wooden table and chair, an old trunk to one side, and some rough shelving on the other wall. It was bitterly cold but at least I was out of the raging gale. I noticed a mouldy loaf and a piece of hard cheese on a high shelf, placed there with a map and an old, ornate compass.

The dog whined. I called out again, gently. 'Bess, Bess, where are you girl?' I wasn't good at illness or injury, and hoped she was not too unwell or hurt too badly. I followed the whines towards the shadows and found her, curled up in the blankets of a bed. She seemed pleased to see me and licked my hand. Pathetically. She was weak and thin.

I held the candle closer to her to check for injuries and reassure her. In doing so, my whole body went rigid with a sudden terrible shock. Bess lay in the arms of my rescuer. There were the eyebrows, the beard, and the old woollen coat.

He had been dead for some time.

Woman to Child

by Anna Newman

Do you know what I would like to do one day?
One day.
I would like to visit myself as a child.

What would I say to her?
Woman to child?
For she seems to inhabit a different world
To my world now.

What common ground surrounds us
For we seem to stand apart?

I can see her,
I can hear her
But I cannot touch her,
I cannot communicate,

For we are cut off by a million experiences
That turned her into me.

(Child to Woman)

Do you know what I would like to do one day?
One day.
I would like to visit myself as a woman.

What would I say to her?
Child to woman?
She is strangely familiar
But totally unknown.

She crouches down to me
And holds out her hands

Her eyes are bright with tears
As she calls my name.

I can see her,
I can hear her
But I cannot touch her
I cannot communicate

For we are cut off by a million experiences
That will turn me into her.

My Child

by Anna Newman

In the bright circle of the world she stood
Star crowned.

She smiled in wonder
Held out her hands
And spun amid the springtime meadows
Spin-dreft with soft, fresh flowers
Rain-washed citrine, sapphire and pink
Sparkling about her.

She smiled with joy
Held out her hands
And danced amid the summer pastures
Hot, verdant, gold and emerald.
She spun in the fiery sky
She was the sun to me.

She smiled with delight
Held out her hands

And danced amid the autumn woods
With crimsons, ambers and antique greens
She swirled around the glancing leaves
In crazy infinity.

She smiled in awe
Held out her hands
And danced amid the winter landscape
With skirling flakes she reeled
Dizzy with ecstasy between the twiggy trees
She tasted heaven on earth

In the bright circle of the world she stood
Star crowned
She was in all the world for me
And all the world was in her
The child I never had.

Colour

by John Cliff

You ask what is my favourite colour.
Now let me think.
That depends on how I'm feeling at the time,
Like 'in the pink.'

Which is not the answer you want.
So, a different hue,
A more masculine choice you may agree
Would be blue.

Neither am I feeling blue right now,
Maybe green.
No, no, I'm not feeling sick at all,
I really mean

Nature's attire in spring and summer
Comes to mind.
In all the shades that greenery holds
Do I find

Them in every leaf and stem or blade
Of vernal grass.
Yet thinking, how can I be forgetting
Autumn's tints; alas

Green cannot hold sway forever, as the gold
Autumnal crown
Enters stage, bejeweled with crimson, yellow
And earth-baked brown.

And dipped in sunlight my brush can paint
Any colour
You or I may wish for, but not the answer you want.
Brighter or duller

Shades can be picked from my musical palette:
A violet hue
For the saddest of tunes, and for uplifting song
A heavenly blue.

But you want to know my favourite colour -
My candid choice.
I'll close my eyes and dip into the rainbow.
Out comes turquoise!

Catbells & Derwentwater

by John Cliff

Dedicated to: Painting in acrylic by James Hall

What is between you and me and the water I see?
The artist's brush demonstrating poise?
There is no music, but a voice
Whispers from the painted horizon
In colourful tone.
The artist is not alone.

Those hills, mysterious shades blended into a haze
Of rapture cast off the palette,
Separated by dancing water, yet
Whispering, beckoning the onlooker
Which is I
Sitting in his cobalt sky.

Beneath the Treetops

by John Cliff

What lies beneath the tree tops in May?
I ask the rooks on sentinel towers.
Pass through, pass through, they seem to say:
The songbird choir has greeted the day,
The pigeons are timing the hours.

As woodpecker hammers on timpani tree,
Messages echo down emerald glade.
Come along, come along, it sounds to me,

Follow the path and listen and see,
For the time is still being made.

The sun-slanted rays are catching the dew
Dissolving in droplets on ferny frond.
Look around, look around at the azure hue
Painted on bluebells; watch life anew
Stirring in green fringed pond.

Skippers and whites and commas in flight,
The butterflies dance in balmy breeze.
Follow closely while the day is still light
Before the owl awakens at night
And the pigeon clock stops in the trees.

I smell May blossom at the woodland edge
With cow parsley frothy and high,
And at the stile by a tangled hedge
A blackbird sings from a stony ledge
His melodious song of goodbye.

Getting to grips with the Garden

from the diary letters by John Cliff

13th March

Yesterday I had a load of slabs, sand, cement and gravel delivered, essential materials for getting to grips with Phase Three of my emergent garden creation. The first part of the plot had been dug out and bagged up out of the way. When one surveys this sort of task in hand, one mentally calculates the number of rubble bags needed to fill with the earth being removed. By multiplying this estimate by three the result is about right. Instead of a single trip to the council tip twelve miles away I had three; no less than seventy-two miles there and back just to dispose of garden rubble. A good three hours wasted leaving one's joints aching and the car complaining. And I thought three was my lucky number.

I should not moan despite the substantial undertaking. Think of when it is all done and I can sit in the warm sunshine, a glass of cool ale in hand, admiring one's triumph in the battle twixt man and clay, taking in a waft of rose perfume here or of lavender there.

The weather has been kind and the warm conditions are perfect for working on the land. Out with the shovel and away with the slabs I say to myself. Ah, easy said but a trifle harder as I wield the shovel and make up a dry mix for bedding in the slabs, then lifting and levelling those obstinate concrete squares into position. But as work progresses the benefits of having a nice paved area instead of moss covered clay are apparent. Beyond this area I have already started cultivating curved beds for planting up later on. With the help of gravel, peat, soil, hard digging and a few verbal exclamations, the almost intractable clay is turning into a reasonable growing medium. I have to put in raised borders to keep the beds in place, but that's another day.

As I sat in the warm sunshine with a mug of coffee, contemplating my next move, I heard a pair of buzzards wheeling in the distance. In the tree at the end of my plot sparrows were squabbling and I knew that spring was getting to grips with nature. Nature was responding and I felt my small contribution in shaping a piece of earth was a part of it.

Daffodils and Leeks

from the diary letters by John Cliff

1st March

A few days break in St. Davids, Pembrokeshire, had been booked for the patron saint's festival and what better place to celebrate the occasion than in the smallest city in Britain which is named after him.

A small place maybe, but quite a lot of things happening: stalls round the market cross selling local produce, school children in dragon attire parading the streets, flower trails, local history and art exhibitions, Welsh country dancing in the City Hall (called a Twmpath), traditional Welsh hymn singing (Cymanfa Ganu) and, of course, services in St. Davids Cathedral. Pennants and flags declared it was a special celebration and vases of bright yellow daffodils beamed from shops and cottage windows.

My good friend Miss Newman had accompanied me and we were both looking forward to doing something a bit different from the norm. Well, last night the lady was in fine fettle for the Twmpath and was up and dancing before you could say dosi-do. Dancers in costume first displayed a few tricky sequences before showing us how to join in with easier steps. Naturally I did my best which I must say was rather tedious. Fortunately we had brought along a bottle of wine which helped imbue a degree of bravado on my part, if not allow my feet a certain dispensation.

St. David's Day dawned bright and sunny. A choral service in the cathedral was followed by a stroll to the new National Park Centre where we joined people gathering eagerly around the St. Davids Stone. The sun was supposed to shine through a hole in an adjacent boulder, its rays to fall on an engraved icon at midday on St. David's Day. We learned it was the first time the sun had come out for this event but it seemed that everybody involved in putting the stones in place had done their sums right.

Afterwards, a small group of us was led on a coastal walk to St. Non's chapel. Traditionally St. Non, the mother of St. David, gave birth to him where the old chapel ruins stand. Apparently tomorrow is St. Non's Day. What a beautiful day for a walk along the cliff tops. The sea was painted in shades of azure, turquoise and slate grey; the cliffs in a multitude of brown, green, grey and reddish hues; along our path yellow gorse was coming into flower.

The highlight of the afternoon was community hymn singing in the Zion Chapel – a Cymanfa Ganu – sung in Welsh with a fair sprinkling of English to help everyone along. Thank heaven we had hymn sheets. Thank heaven, too, there was no long sermon in Welsh. I am sure for the minority, including ourselves, pronunciation was a matter of trial and error, mostly the latter, although inadequacy of language was swallowed up by rousing song from a chapel packed to the rafters, culminating with the Welsh National Anthem. How thoughtful, and rather civilised too, to have tea waiting at the City Hall for lubricating one's vocal chords.

Indeed, we had taken advantage of plentiful traditional Welsh food. Bara brith and Welsh tea cakes went down a treat, so did cawl – a kind of lamb stew-cum-soup which was superb. But strangest of all was a board outside a shop advertising daffodil and leek ice-cream. Having rather adventurous taste buds this was something I just had to try. Daffodils? Leeks? Was it real? I was assured by the lady scooping up pale yellow and creamy brown balls into a twin cone that it was. I was also comforted in the knowledge that the daffodil part was from the flowers only. Well, I can honestly say a tentative lick from each did not turn me yellow or green. A hint of caramelised onion on the one side did not overpower the light floral tones on the other. Honest!

As the proverb says, "Nid aur yw popeth melyn." (All that glitters is not gold)

Anybody Want a Greyhound?

by Anna Newman

Baggage is a greyhound
A four legged crime wave
If human she would have been
An inmate of Holloway
Merciless!

She would have started off with shoplifting
As a puppy
And worked her way up to bank busting
And worse!

Her covetous eyes are on
My hens, my lunch, my dinner.
She has no morals
No conscience

Baggage is sly, cunning and stealthy.
Fagin would have welcomed her into his den!
Baggage is a nuisance,
A whingeing, whining, reprobate
Who steals whatever she can.

When exhausted from these misdeeds
She stalks off to the settee to rest,

Her legs in the air like a bundle of sticks,
Her head twisted sideways over the edge
But
One eye open for the main chance.

Alas, I am stuck with her forever
God has no place in heaven for a bad dog like her.
She would steal harps and nibble angels' toes.

And the devil? Well he won't have her either,
Warming herself in front of his fire, taking up all the room
No, far better for him if Baggage stays here –
His top agent on earth!

A Short Story in Blank Verse

by Anna Newman

She stared blankly at the blank page
And
The blank page stared blankly back
Which was odd
Because
Behind the blankness was a life crammed with
People, piled up high,
Event after event, pushing and seething with
Betrayals, heartbreaks, sacrifices and angst.

But not joy she noted curiously,
Not much joy
Only the joy she made for herself
No-one gave her joy.

She ought to be able to write
Why couldn't she write?
It was only a short story for goodness sake!
Her life was short stories, one after another, tumbling back to
Her birth
Like giddy dominoes…

Soon, if she didn't do something
Positive,
Creative
Important
Her whole life would be a short story
And over

It would be short because
Nobody
At all
Had told her that she could
Had told her it was possible
Had given her permission
To be herself.

But what if she dared to write what she felt?
What then?
She could hear the mockery from down the years
Pointless,
Talentless,
Mediocre
The voices snuffing out every idea
Every tiny creative flame
Strangled
Like an unwanted kitten.

It was just that she needed now
One person
Just one
A stranger, especially a stranger
To say
OK, it's OK, keep going, work at it
You really do have a voice
You can write
And then that voice
Faintly
Would perhaps
Become words on a page
The blank page
That was once this piece of paper…

The Mithras Inheritance

by Anna Newman

March 15th

Llangellert – just what I need – a small, quiet seaside town, isolated in a shallow valley on a peninsula of towering, brooding cliffs, miles from anywhere – miles from my old life. The digs are ok, neat, tidy – with a sash window looking out onto a cobbled side street. They'll do. Shouldn't think much happens around here – which is odd because I am now the only full-time reporter on the local rag, The Llangellert Times. There's just the editor and an occasional freelance.

I suppose I'd better take a look around my new patch: the pub might be a good place to start, get the local gossip and find out who runs the town. I don't intend to be over friendly though, I don't want to have to explain my past, the miserable divorce, and my kids being kept from me. She's with another man now. Wonder how long it'll be before they call him Dad?

March 16th

I've started at the paper. Seems there's more going on than I thought. I'm supposed to cover everything, news and all the clubs and groups. Had a scintillating morning with the Llangellert Ladies Embroidery Guild. At least the tea and cake made up for it a bit. And a more interesting one with the local rugby club, who were training for their next match. Apparently, they've got a star player. Jim Hunt, being head-hunted by the county team. Got an Archaeological Society meeting to cover tonight – there's talk of a dig up at some cliff top where there are apparently Roman temple remains under a chapel ruin.

March 20th

Turning out to be a busy week. A burglary by some acne-faced yobbo from the next town along the coast, the opening of a new café/tea room in the High Street, and a suicide – a middle-aged teacher from inland, who threw herself off Mithras Cliff. Near the proposed archaeological dig actually. She was said to be depressed because of Ofsted visiting her school, couldn't take the pressure. Talking of pressure, I had a text from my ex-wife saying that she and that man are intending to take the kids away to France for the whole of their summer holidays. Great.

March 22nd

Had a chat in The Baker's Arms with the local self-styled historian. He reckoned that the suicide near those remains was suspect on account of the Roman Temple legend. Something about Mithras and Initiation Rites. Didn't enquire what: some people will make something out of nothing just to get attention. I have plenty more to do, jumble sales, a local auction and a new minister at the chapel. Well one of the chapels.

March 28th

Another suicide! Good God, this place seems a magnet for people wanting to end it all. A young boy this time, in exactly the same place as the woman. He'd had a row with his girlfriend, thought she was seeing someone else. He threw himself off the cliffs onto some pretty sharp rocks below. They don't know yet whether death was instantaneous, or whether he bled to death or drowned. What a waste. I could have told him that if his girlfriend had been cheating on him, he'd had a lucky break finding out when he did – unlike me – who found out too late.

April 10th

Been too busy to write in this diary lately. My bloody ex has left me a message with the landlady saying she and the kids are going to Alton Towers this weekend, my weekend to visit them. Haven't seen them for months now. She's even returned Connor's birthday card and present, unopened. Going out to drown my sorrows.

April 11th

All I can see in my mind's eye is those kids at Alton Towers. And Connor thinking that I had forgotten his birthday.

April 13th

Jim Hunt is dead! The local rugby star. He was only eighteen.

Everybody is stunned, especially as he was found on the same rocks as the other two. What is this for God's sake? Viral suicide? I hope it's not catching.

April 14th

All the talk is of Jim Hunt and the local legend. Some ancient chap in The Baker's Arms was going on about how that Roman Temple was dedicated to Mithras and how they had initiation ceremonies up there on the cliff top, pretending to push people off but holding them back at the last second. To test their nerves they said. Bloody hell fire! All the same it does seem odd, all this suicide stuff in the same place. Wonder if it's a mass hysteria thing?

Weather turning very rough lately and storms predicted for the next few days. Expect I'll be covering the Jim Hunt inquest in due course. No-one can think of a single reason why he jumped.

April 16th

Got nothing much on this weekend – just a wedding on Saturday morning – which I am obviously not in the mood for. Nothing after that.

April 17th

Well that's the wedding done, thank God. Kept thinking of mine, kept going over what went wrong. Kept thinking that if I'd paid her more attention she might not have…but that's all gone now. I had to work hard to keep us all. Now I've lost everything.

Later: curiosity has got the better of me. What is it about that place that prompts people to commit suicide? Some long-dead priest pushing them over and not catching them? As if. Crumbling cliff edges, the wind? Or simply depression for whatever reason? Desperate enough to kill themselves but sane enough to select that site for the deed? Who knows?

Decided to go up to that cliff top temple place anyway. And take some sandwiches to eat in the chapel ruin. Should be enough shelter there. The wind is getting up and it's raining, but I've got my stout boots and all my wet weather gear.

Later still: had my lunch sitting on the old stones, hunched up against the weather. It's worsening now, and the rain has got in places where rain has no business to be. I've looked at the edge. It's pretty scary. There's a lot of loose rock and soil. I had to step back pretty smartly on a couple of occasions. The rocks below look – are – lethal. Wonder what it feels like as your body is impaled on the razor like slate teeth? God help me. I think of my kids suddenly and how they would love it here in the summer. My kids…I'm beginning to understand why people choose not to live…

Nearly dusk now…I've got the beginnings of an idea for an article on all this for one of the nationals. Made some notes etc., but the ink is running on the paper with the rain. Will get back soon…The atmosphere has thickened here, must be that legend getting on my nerves. Time to go.

Dusk…the storm is here, a vicious off-shore gale and lashing, stinging rain. Must get back very soon…first will take one more look over the edge. Carefully. Can't get rid of the feeling that I should be looking over my shoulder…to see what? I don't know.

The Llangellert Times. Copy for lead article May 9th

The inquest on the death of Mark Weston, late reporter on this newspaper, was held today at the Town Hall. Mr Weston's body was found on the Mithras Rocks on 18th April by a couple walking their dogs. The Coroner, after due consideration, returned an open verdict. Full story inside.

A Season in Time

from the diary letters of John Cliff

1st May

The birds were noisier than usual this morning and were extremely active as if they were preparing for a special occasion which had only just been brought to their notice, or which they had overlooked during their preoccupation with mating and nest-building. The small rookery at the end of the lane was likewise the subject of great noise and activity. Yet on close observation one would concur that all the cacophony was for show. There was no sign of anything actually being done. Was it a ritual we humans are obliged to be excluded from and not supposed to know about? But then on further observation one is conscious of a distinct change in the surroundings as though in the night, as one slept unawares, nature had taken out her paintbrushes and daubed more green on the trees and hedgerows , added a few splashes of white along the hawthorn, stroked the violets with colour and given another coat of yellow to the dandelions. She had found a few spaces among the trees to adorn with blue and mauve bells and little white stars.

Surely it was different yesterday when one could see clearly through the tree tops and marvel at the emerging leaves of hazel, wych elm and field maple, when the blackbird scurried in the soft earth and looked about in leisurely fashion. Even then the rooks were only grumbling quietly to themselves as they rearranged a twig or two in their nests. But was it yesterday? Was it not last week, or the week before? One feels the Book of Time has cheated on us and hidden our eyes from a chapter.

It is said that Time passes more quickly as one gets older. Of course it does not; it is we who are tricked by his insinuations. Is it Time who rules the seasons and who tells Nature when to take out her paint box? One imagines that Nature in her turn can tell Time a thing or two and it seems today she has scolded him for dragging his feet.

Then I mentioned, in an earlier letter, a rumour to the effect that winter will merge into summer with hardly any spring in between. Naturally I dismissed this as pure tittle-tattle but I am now thinking there may be a grain of truth in it.

I shall return to the garden and crack on with summer bedding and put up the bean sticks smartish. Summer is beckoning and time is in short supply.

Words of Fashion

from the diary letters of John Cliff

12th May

The English language has such a rich and complex history that one frequently comes up against a new word, which in fact could be an old word in the sense that it is rarely used nowadays or describes some peculiar obsolescence. However, one may suspect there is another source of words emanating from female fashion pundits.

During a tour of an impressive late 18th century house in Shropshire, owned by the National Trust, I was admiring one of the many rooms when a young lady brushed past me whose unexpected presence and attire caused me to utter within earshot, 'Oh, a maid!' The lady, who was leading another tour, replied indignantly, 'A maid?' My somewhat involuntary outburst was quite without foundation. Who would see a maid dressed from head to toe in someone's curtains, I asked myself. Her head was adorned with a substantial hat and from her arm hung a tiny handbag, all in the same floral patterned material as her dress.

Fortunately I was accompanied by my close and learned friend, Miss Newman, who gently reprimanded me in my ignorance, explaining that the guide was not wearing curtains or carrying a handbag. The accessory suspended from her arm was in fact a reticule and the hat was a mob cap, replicating costume of the Regency period. Miss Newman is well versed in historical matters so one should take particular notice and pay deference to her valuable contribution to one's knowledge. In my defence, however, I knew that in botanical circles the Latin term reticulata is suffixed to at least one plant in my garden, that small early flowering Iris. One could assume that the lady's reticule has something to do with that, although I did not recall seeing any irises on the curtains.

Retail therapy is de rigueur with Miss Newman and on one such occasion we happened to amble through a maze of women's accessories in a large store. I found myself in the hat department and immediately came across feathered oddities befitting a young Indian squaw or someone intent on ornithological pursuits. My puzzlement was immediately dismissed as my learned friend introduced me to the Fascinator, an item of headgear worn as a substitute for a proper hat, rather useful, one would think, if the wearer has to pass through revolving doors. In the same store I was led through a more intimate part which displayed from every corner an array of ladies exotic underwear, where a man feels he might be more comfortable in the book department. I was shown a piece of apparel called a Bustier (French pronunciation but obvious where it fits), yet another, a Basque.

One could imagine fashion and design gurus dreaming up new descriptions with each snip of the scissors.

A Reunion, Roses, Victoriana and a Fiendish Hill

from the diary letters of John Cliff

10th June

Two days ago saw the arrival of friends from Bridlington. Only last year did I meet them for the first time in over thirty years when I was invited to their home on the east coast of Yorkshire. It was almost a coincidence following a casual remark by an old work colleague on the internet that led to my being given the contact details of Peter and Christine. Since then we have exchanged correspondence on a regular basis.

Yesterday we decided to take off for a famous rose nursery near here. Like myself, Christine is particularly fond of these old English roses and it is a good time to see many varieties coming into bloom. I had arranged for us to meet Miss Newman at the nursery. After we had concluded introductions at the entrance we ambled into the gardens for a preliminary look round before having lunch in the restaurant. Peter and myself were hard pressed to match the vociferous chat between the two ladies, although we did our best.

It had been a day of uncertain weather. March emerged with a stiff breeze to do battle with April's showers, then May showed up at half time knocking at the season's door to tell June to be up and about. Nevertheless, the rose gardens were producing plentiful colour and perfume, even though they would not be at their best for another three weeks. The afternoon brought more sunshine as we admired the plant sales area. Our friends told us they have a 'Rambling Rector' festooning a shed in their garden. As they are actively involved with their local church I thought it a most fitting choice.

Miss Newman had to leave us when we came away from the nursery but joined us this evening for a dinner in Ironbridge, after I had shown Peter and Christine around a Victorian village on a historical industrial site, a living museum recreating many interesting sights of that era. Our first call was at the old bank which fascinated Peter because he used to be a bank manager. We meandered along the streets, into Victorian style shops, a colliery winding house, candle maker, forge, bakery, surgery and so on, finding time to have a light lunch in a Victorian tea room.

The venue for our evening meal was a pub overlooking the river, accessed by numerous steps from the car park.. As Peter's disability prevented him from climbing so much, the landlord directed me to another access via a circular route from a higher road to approach the pub down a very steep hill. One would consider it to be a bit of an understatement. The one-in-four-cum-one-in-three precipitous descent was a hair-raising experience. Applying the brakes would have little effect should one meet a vehicle coming upwards, if a vehicle is capable of doing so. But then one could not imagine anybody wanting to walk up, let alone drive. Thank goodness Peter was able to descend the steps after our meal.

Tomorrow my guests are returning home after a few enjoyable days in Shropshire. We shall obviously meet up again, maybe next time in Bridlington, but have agreed not to leave it for another thirty-odd years.

Over Brown Clee

by John Cliff

Here I rest upon Brown Clee Hill,
From where I peer into an azure sky
Watching kestrels, motionless on wing,
Before they swoop beyond my viewing eye.

The sun is warm, an imperceptible breeze
Is acknowledged by feather headed grasses
Nodding lightly, yet within entwined arms
Of an old hedgerow no movement passes.

Before me, westward, unfolds a panorama
As English as England could prepare
Upon a pastoral canvas: diverse hues
Of green and gold paint Corvedale fair.

Did Housman seek this very place and feel
As I, a quickening heart? Oh, pleasure fills
The artist's soul, a palette of life and colour
To cast upon those blue remembered hills.

Down, down I go from Shropshire's rooftop
Where Abdon's rivulet twists and creeps
Through summery glades, and I, likewise on
Twisting lane, find Clee St. Margaret sleeps.

Slumbering within shady sandstone walls,
Safe by the hill whose name you share,
Only birdsong and your gurgling street ford
Announces my presence, that I called there.

I paddle through the cooling stream of Clee
And find a place of softly dappled hue.

In the flickering sunlight of a leafy fold
In sleepy Clee St. Margaret, I slumber too.

Birds

by Anna Newman

They were dead
Three sodden lumps of feathers
Once full of glancing movement
And bright eyes, demanding beaks.
Now lying on the forest floor
Surrounded by the mossy remains of their woody stronghold
Dashed to oblivion by the impartial fury of a storm.

If I were God, I thought,
I could not let that happen
If I, imperfect mortal, could feel
That stab of compassion,
Ripping my heart like a knife,
It begged the question
Of how God felt about his own creation.

Perhaps it is a question too painful to ask
Perhaps I could not bear the answer.

The Fairy Flies

by John Cliff

Flies, you may conclude, are nasty,
Especially when they settle
Upon your Cornish Pasty
And lick the gravy from the rim
Of the nice white dinner plate.
A vile habit, so awfully grim.

Uncouth insects are not for me
Because I'll tell you where to see
Gyrating 'neath the summer skies
Myriads of fairy flies.

There, quietly by the water's edge,
Performing acrobatics in the sedge
On delicate wings of finest lace,
Alighting with the utmost grace
Upon the loosestrife pink.

Look, fluorescent damsels link
As they dart through the reeds
Flashing flamboyant beads
Of blue and green and brown.

I turn around to see
An alder land upon my knee.
(This rather smart and friendly fly
Thought he'd call on passing by).

I turn again, for now I've seen
The summer waters' hatching queen

Of fairy flies: the Mayfly floating down
The crystal glide;
Then another and a dozen more,
And a hundred fairies rise,
Softly lifting to the skies.

Hundreds more - the air's alive
With Mayflies spinning, dancing,
Inebriated by summer sun.
But, oh, too soon to end their fun;
Touching the cooling stream,
Quelling a fairy fly's dream
In a moment of frenzy.

There, lurking 'neath the glassy flow
Salmo trutta will certainly know
When fairy flies exhausted drop,
Dinner is served.

Plop! Plop! Plop!

August Moon in the Greenhouse

by John Cliff

I always wanted to sleep in the greenhouse. Granddad's especially. It was very big with pipes inside to keep it warm in winter. Strange that I dreamt about it once, all those years ago when I was of an impressionable age, a stripling as we used to say. Often I stayed with my grandparents for a weekend and from my bedroom window I had a view of the greenhouse and all of the garden down to the fields. There were apple and damson trees, soft fruit shrubs, vegetables, all kinds of flowers. A giant rhubarb lived outside the back of the greenhouse which I used to hide behind when running around the myriad connecting paths. Sometimes granddad shouted at me for being wild. Out of breath I would then lie in the sunshine on the lawn surrounded by rose shrubs, backed by a wall on which a pear tree was trained along wires.

Of course there were fairies at the bottom of the garden. There had to be. They danced with the butterflies in the nettles and cow parsley in spring – just over the hawthorn hedge. In summer they brushed the grasses to make pollen dust while counting time on dandelion clocks. I never actually saw them but I found their tiny footprints by the shed where they slept at night. Granddad said it was only the cat but I told him it was a secret between the cat and myself, so there!

If only I could sleep in the greenhouse. I talked to cat about it one night, who returned a scowl as if to say it wasn't my place. He was a tabby and obviously not as clever as a black cat who knew witches – they could do magic. I bet they could take me to the fairies, and the greenhouse at night. When cat became bored with my questions he yawned and coiled up on the end of the bed. The moon had come up and was casting a vaporous light through the net curtains onto the rose-patterned wallpaper. I half rolled on the bed to look outside. The greenhouse was shimmering in the moonlight.

Suddenly cat sprang up from his nap and almost threw himself at the window, making an awful din, as if he had seen something. I put my head to the glass as cat ran around the bedroom; a bit frightening, I can tell you. Opening the window enough to take a peek I noticed a shadow settle on top of the garden wall below. Cat stopped his antics, jumped on the bed and coiled up again.

'You!' A croaky voice came from the shadow.

'Who is it? I replied, rather hesitantly.

'You dreamin', boy?'

'What?' I answered.

'Dreamin. You wanna sleep in the greenhouse, don't you?'

'Er… yes... b... but how do you know?' Oddly, I wasn't as scared as cat was.

'Look, we've not got a lot of time, boy. You're lucky to be chosen.'

'Chosen?'

'First full moon in August is the night and that's tonight, boy. Pulled your name out of the hat. My hat!'

'Who are you?'

'Mirabelle. I'm comin up.'

I fell back onto the bed as a figure leapt onto the window ledge. It held a broomstick and wore a pointy hat. The window opened another few inches.

'Your cat ain't compatible with mine, so I've put a spell on him. He'll sleep till mornin.'

'Where's yours?' I asked.

'Playin' wi' the fairies, the silly bugger. Oh, sorry, boy, I oughtn't swear, not in my position.'

'What's that?'

'As chief gusgog witch, Mirabelle 'as to be impeccable.'

'I've never heard of you.'

'You won't, 'cos you only hear when your name is pulled out o' my 'at, see.'

I was feeling too sleepy to be scared as the witch put her legs over the inside of the window sill, straightened her hat and stood her broomstick against the wall. She wore green striped trousers and a brown hairy cloak. Her long boots were old and wrinkly like her partly hidden face which didn't look at all nasty.

'First,' she said, 'close your eyes and think about the greenhouse. Then we're off.'

'I .....I can't fly.'

'Who said anything about flyin', boy. You do it by thinkin.'

'Oh, so I close my eyes and think, do I?'

'That's what I said, so hurry up and I'll tell you when to open them.'

I closed my eyes and thought very hard about the greenhouse and how much I'd like to be asleep in there among the tomatoes and geraniums and the smell of warm damp earth and the ......

'Open yer eyes now .' The voice interrupted my thoughts. I saw the pink roses on the wallpaper yet I was looking through, between them. I was on my bed with cat asleep at the end, a cloud of silver moonlight carpeting the floor, yet the greenhouse was all around, enveloping me in soft fragrances and hues. .

'There we are. Didn't hurt a bit, eh!'

I could barely speak. The gusgog witch continued:

'Now, I've got work to do. Where's me basket? '

She picked up a wicker basket with a long strap which she flung over her shoulder. Astride the broomstick she disappeared through the glass. Nothing shattered, not even the silence. I must have fallen asleep because I dreamt of seeing fairies flying in the greenhouse, swinging from the plants, sliding down the leaves, polishing the tomatoes to make them turn red. A black cat was trying to catch them but never got close enough. They teased it by swinging on its tail. I thought I heard a baby's cry, or maybe it was a bird of the night . A dark shape flew overhead but it wasn't an owl; it was a … a… witch. Mirabelle was back. She put down the basket and broomstick, removed her pointy hat and sat on an upturned bucket. I was curious about the basket.

'Hello,' I greeted her vaguely, dreamlike.

'You want to know what's in me basket, eh?'

'Please'.

'Do you like gusgogs?' She pulled a gooseberry from a pocket in her cloak

'Not a lot,' I answered.

'Good in pies, I've 'eard. I eats 'em at work.'

'Work?' I queried.

'Now, boy, you 'ave to learn about the birds and the bees one day, but let me tell you, what's in my basket ain't nothing like you might be told. A gusgog witch is experienced in such matters.'

I knew it was a dream and I knew nothing of what she was talking about. There were gooseberry bushes in the garden and the berries gave me tummy ache. I certainly knew that. 'So you've been picking granddad's gooseberries, then? You must have a basket full.'

She placed the basket before me. There was a blanket over the top. I lifted a corner and saw a tiny face which turned and grinned.

'A baby!' I gasped

'What you expect, boy. The reason being all babies are found under gooseberry bushes. I see to that. It's my job. Then I takes 'em in me basket to their mothers. Simple, ain't it! Thought you might 'ave known.'

Mirabelle chomped noisily on a gooseberry. Her teeth weren't very nice. I was confused. I had never seen any sign of a baby under granddad's gooseberries. He hadn't told me anything about that.

'Now, I 'ave to take this last one to the nursing 'ome pronto. Due at five thirty in the morning, on the dot.'

Then I saw that the fairies were fading. Their bodies were hazy, nearly transparent, as they drifted over the foliage and scooped up the moonlight around my bed. They were like moths. A bumble bee appeared from the haze. Mirabelle touched it with a long finger and it suddenly turned into a black cat, purring by her side.

Mirabelle spoke to it. 'You never learn, Figaro, do you. You can't catch then fairies, but they catches you an' turns you into a bee.'

I saw the witch's face more clearly and it reminded me of great-grandma's sepia photograph hanging in its frame on the bedroom wall, apart from the teeth, that is.

Mirabelle looked up and sighed. 'Gotta go, boy. 'Ope you liked being picked out of me 'at. Always gives me pleasure to see young'ns enjoy a bit of magic. I gets all emotional when I looks at the gusgogs an' the babies an' thinks one of their names could be on a piece of paper in me 'at one August moon.'

The witch's face lit up and I saw her smile. I think I saw a tear in her eye.

'Nice knowin' you, boy.'

'Will I see you again ?' I paused. 'Er, Mirabelle.'

'Depends on 'ow you think. Keep your mind open when you looks for fairies at the bottom of the garden. 'Eard you talking to them once, I did. Now close your eyes, boy.'

I closed them and with a lump in my throat wondered how I would get back to the house. What if the door was locked? How would I creep upstairs.? Where's cat? Oh, dear! I sat up, breathless, eyes wide open, pink roses wallpaper in front of me. My bedroom window was slightly open as it had been left in the night. The moon was a circle of fine lace over a pale blue morning sky. The sun had come up. I got out of bed and rubbed my eyes before walking over to the photo of great-grandma. As I touched her face a beam of sunlight shone onto it and a breeze stirred the net curtains when I turned to the window.

At the breakfast table, granddad shook his head as he poured milk onto his cornflakes. He looked at grandma. 'Dear,' he said, 'I can't understand how cat came to be in the greenhouse when I opened up this morning. Everything was all shut up last night as usual. And another thing.'

'Yes, Arthur.' Grandma raised her eyebrows as Granddad continued.

'I walked down the garden and found gooseberries had been picked and left on the ground. And why the blazes do I find safety pins hanging on the branches, I ask you.'

Grandma, in her gentle manner, faced me and said, 'John, did you hear anything strange last night.'

'Nothing, Grandma.'

She looked towards Granddad. 'Do you think we had a visitor?'

'Hmm,' was the only answer as he scooped up his cornflakes.

Grandma gave me a wink. She hadn't done that before

A Boyhood Dream

by John Cliff

The picture opens on a summer's day, school holidays and a small boy leaning on a wooden fence in a sunny space between a boundary of wych elm, hawthorn and elder, notebook with dog-eared corners and a pencil in hand, casting his eyes up and down the railway lines facing him. There may have been an official walkway across the railway track to a gate on the opposite side. He doesn't remember, for now this boy is well over three score years older. But he clearly sees the hard sinews of steel stretching into infinity, reflecting the afternoon sunshine. Infinity was Derby one way and Nottingham the other. If the memory has not become distorted with age he was visualising five or six pairs of track and maybe a siding to cross to the other side. He imagines that it was not an official crossing.

A couple of friends join him, John Kidger, a fishing pal and another lad, all about the same age, wearing short trousers and grubby short-sleeved shirts, feet stuck inside pumps or sandals. They, too, are armed with the essentials of train spotting - the ubiquitous notebook and pencil. There is a ringing in the silver rails, the first sign of an approaching train. The ringing gets louder, before the steel serpent, locked onto its sleepers hisses and vibrates as iron and steel thunder over it and three boys freeze momentarily watching the express hurry by. "Nottingham quick - Nottingham quick - Nottingham quick" the train is saying as the number 43106 is entered into each notebook. It was a Stanier locomotive, big, assertive and shiny black. Suddenly silence again as the ringing of the rails fades away and is replaced by the sound of sparrows chirping in the hedgerow.

'Been down the river, Kidge?'

'Yeah, went yesterday. Only got a few minnows, though.'

'What about us going to the canal tomorrow.'

'Can't, got to go shopping with Mum.' Gran's coming over from Long Eaton.

'Oh.'

'I'm OK for Sat'day.'

'Good, meet you by the bridge.'

The discussion is interrupted by the appearance of a slow goods train, quietly going about its business on the far side. A small 0-6-0 shunter puffs away calmly, ignoring the clatter of wagons in tow. Rattling chains and squeaking wheels join the ceaseless melody of sparrows in a cacophony of dissonance: symphonic variations for trainspotters. The unmistakeable aroma of smoke and steam pervades the afternoon stillness.

'I've got that one: seen it a few times. Look, on this page. Bet it's from Chaddesden sidings.'

The picture is expanded when the slow up train leaves Spondon station grunting as it gathers momentum, enveloped in a cloud of smoke and steam.

'Must be the 3.45 to Derby. What's the engine?'

'Dunno, can't see for steam.'

'Is it a namer?'

'Don't get namers on this one.'

The three lads squint in the sunlight in an attempt to penetrate the veil of vapour licking the footplate.

'Couldn't get it. What about you?'

'No, but looks like the usual.'

'Ay, anybody got an 'apenny in their pocket?'

'What for?'

'We could squash it on the line.'

'Ay, yes, I've got one.'

The goods train was still creeping towards Spondon, destined for the Celanese sidings.

'When's the next train due?'

'Reckon it's the London express.'

'Shall we put the 'apenny on the line..

'Who's goin' to do it?'

'Me. It's all clear.'

One of us tosses over the fence rail and walks to the first main line, looks about him, then places the coin on it and runs back, this time squeezing under the fence rail as a man in blue overalls and a peaked railway cap comes into view crossing the lines from the other side. They look at each other. He doesn't see the coin. 'Hello,' he half smiles as the boys move out of the way to let him through.

'When's the train due? I want a pee.'

'And me.'

'Yeah, me too. No sound yet. Should be ten minutes.'

As the necessity for relief had infected them simultaneously, they promptly shuffled into line in a depression by the wych elm. Someone exclaims, 'Phew, I was burstin.' They regained their position at the fence. Kidge was trying to push out the pith from a piece of elder he had broken off. The other friend was sharpening his pencil on a broken brick. One boy stood on the fence and leant over, ears tuned to the permanent way.

'Something's coming.' The others stopped what they were doing and joined him. The rails began their metallic whoosh and a rumble grew in the distance. They clambered over to the fence for a better view. A pall of smoke revealed the whereabouts of the oncoming train.

'It might be a double-header. Enough smoke.' Yes, got to be. Get your books ready.'

The train approached at moderate speed, enabling them to gape at the coupled locomotives hauling a long snake of maroon and cream coaches. 'Hey, it's 'Prestatyn' at the front, with 5517. I haven't got these. What about you two. '

'Saw 5517 last year, but not the namer. Wow, this'll make Phil jealous when he's back off holiday. Two Patriots together. Ha-ha! Let's have a look at the 'apenny.' They stuff their notebooks and pencils into back pockets.

The three sprint to the line. A distorted piece of thin metal lies where it had been left, almost twice its original size.

'Can't spend this.' Each examined the result closely, trying to bend it, feeling the uneven edge, holding it up as if they had discovered a rare coin from Roman Derventio. A signal alarmed them as it clattered back to neutral. They ran to the fence and rolled over the top.

'Got to go now.'

'An' me. See you Sat'day.'

Kidge and friend half-skipped along the dusty road to the prefabs. A hooter blew from the Celanese. Knocking-off time. Might catch up with dad when he leaves work, the small boy thought as he hopped along the dry lane past a discarded rusty pram, leaping potholes and kicking pieces of rubble. He comes out onto a roadway which takes him to the Celanese gates and the railway crossing. Hanging around where workers escape in profusion from the works exit, he looks out for dad and spots him in the crowd. Everybody waits at the level crossing for a train to leave the station. The gates open and they all plough across up the road over the canal bridge. Dad stops to light his pipe and the son looks over the bridge into the clear water. A large pike is basking in a reedy fringe by some willows. He's saying to himself, "I'm going to try for him on Saturday."

Six or seven years later the same small boy, now a teenager, begins his first job as booking and parcels office clerk at Ambergate station. He is initiated by Ted, the chief clerk, and is gradually introduced to the secrets of railway doctrines and practices. The station master is a kindly man who lives in a large house up a long drive at the back of the station. The new starter is rather nervous, especially when invited for tea with the station master and his wife. The booking office is small and cosy. A lot of railway paraphernalia lies on shelves and in drawers which the new employee has to learn about. There are ledgers to be written up, tickets to be sold, tea to brew. He learns how to release racing pigeons from the baskets which come off some trains. He is privileged to enter a signal box and pull a signal for a non-stop express train. There is so much more.

All memories. I never did catch that pike.

Champagne Charlie

by Anna Newman

Y'know, I were thinking back t'other day about the old times. Life were grand here in Shelford then. It were all ok until the70's like. Now the 60's, they'd passed us by pretty well, nowt changed much. Come the 70's life went a bit downhill for me and never properly picked up again.

It started with me job, we were on strike at colliery and long and short of it I found meself out of work for the first time in me life. But me wife, Doris, blow me, she went out and got a job all by 'erself! Seemed all upside down like, me kicking around at 'ome and 'er out earning money. Didn't seem natural.

That weren't all. The country was fair going to dogs, what with cod wars and hijackers and such like. Then what should happen but me old drinking pub, the Miners' Arms, gets taken over by one of these upstart companies, 'ell bent on modernising it. Nearly did for me that did. They ripped it apart, no more darts or dominoes, and put in all these plastic stools and glass panels everywhere. Broke me heart to see all that 'istory ruined.

'Why don't you just try it?' Doris said to me, but I said 'Not likely, you won't catch me in that poncy place, not for a long time.'

She said, 'Oh, go on, let's try it. It might be good.'

So bloody 'ell, there was I, out drinking with me wife and daughter, just to shut her up a bit. I'm used to a man's pub, me, honest and down to earth, drinking with me mates, not with bloody women.

Me daughter, Sal, she were just eighteen then, she came downstairs looking like a bloody gipsy. 'There's enough material in that skirt,' I said. 'To make a new set of curtains for our double bay.' And beads in her hair! 'What are you?' I said. 'Bloody Minnie Ha-ha? First you wear skirts that look like pelmets and now you go to opposite extremes. I don't understand, I don't.'

She flounced down, taking no notice of me, her dad, and told me I were behind the times and it were all flower power now.

Well, we went off to Miner's, didn't we? Except it's renamed The Eagle now. Never seen a bloody eagle around here in all me life! Who thinks these things up? We goes in and Sal gets all smiley and girly and tosses 'er 'air, which looks like it's had a row with a blunt lawnmower. All because there's this lad behind bar, shaking bloody cocktails. I ask you!

I ordered Doris and Sal their Babychams and tried to get a decent pint of beer. Well, you'd have thought I asked for the moon. In the end Doris told me to stop my grumbling and order a Tequila Sunrise. A tequila bloody surprise more like it. That's what comes of drinking with bloody women. I made do with a lager.

I soon noticed Sal were taken with barman. Bloody sight he was, hair down to 'is shoulders for a start. And, my God what he were wearing! A great loose shirt and embroidered, yes embroidered bloody trousers. Sal said they were jeans, Dad. I told her they were a bloody disgrace.

Anyway we stayed for a bit until I couldn't stomach it any more.

'I'm off to Working Men's Club,' I shouted. 'Where they've got real ale served by real men.' And this barman, Charlie was his name, he put up two fingers at me and said 'peace and love, Dad.'

'I'm not your bloody Dad, thank God,' says I. Peace and love indeed. And I left Doris and Sal there, talking to this long streak of lightning in his women's gear.

Our Sal took up with this lad. Doris was smitten too, inviting him home to tea. He was all glamour to our Sal, he talked about going to San Francisco and wearing flowers in his hair and the like. Saying that all we need is peace and love.

'You can't pay your bills with peace and love,' says I. 'And you can clear off to bloody San Francisco soon as yer like.'

He says, 'No worries man. Live and let live.'

Well I didn't take to him at all, lazy article he was. And never 'ad any money, spent all his wages on drink and drugs. Sal, though, was bowled over by him, and she was getting into bad ways with all this free love stuff. I knowed she give him money too. Bloody parasite. I told him, 'Get a haircut and join the forces, they might make a man of you.'

He said he didn't believe in fighting and suchlike, only goodness and harmony.

'That's no way for a man to talk,' says I.

He was shifty too, always seemed to be lurking around where he shouldn't be in the house. Doris, she lost a couple of fivers at that time, though I couldn't prove nothing. Time proved me right though. Talk about the shame of it. One day he was supposed to take our Sal to some pop festival and he didn't turn up. What a state she was in, crying and all. I told her bloody good riddance and said I hoped he would come back.

Doris said, 'You're upsetting her, leave her alone. He might have had an accident or something.'

We found out later, my mate being the local constable, this Charlie had flitted off from The Eagle after stealing a cheque and a crate of Champagne. He'd scarpered right enough. And – this really upset me – it turned out later that he secretly contacted our Sal and she hid him in bloody garden shed for two weeks. That's where the police found him, sitting cross-legged and smoking this pot stuff and leaning on the crate of Champagne. And he'd got our Sal to cash the cheque he'd tampered with. The bloody shame of it. I cried. A grown man, hard as you like and I cried. We'd brought our Sal up decent like, so we thought.

Anyway, after a bit they went to court and got suspended sentences.

'I'd like to suspend him,' I said afterwards. 'Up a bloody tree.'

But Doris said, 'Give the lad a chance for Sal's sake.'

I said, 'What's that supposed to mean? She can't want to carry on with him now, not after him bringing bloody disgrace on us?'

I can still see the looks between Charlie and Doris and Sal.

'What?' I said again. 'What's going on? You're a waster,' I told him. 'Stealing bloody Champagne, what's the point of stealing bloody champagne? Anybody'd think you got something to celebrate.'

'We have, Dad,' says my Sal. 'I'm pregnant.'

I were never the same after that, I can tell you, with that idle no-good as my son-in-law. Oh, he tried to get round me. And I suppose he did get a proper job in the end. He's not got into trouble again, so far as I know. But he 'ad the last laugh on me, he did. To go and crown it all they go and christen my grandchildren Summer Sky and Moonlight Star. Moonlight Star is my bloody grandson! Imagine if you were out with him and people say, what a nice lad. He your grandson? What's his name?

Moonlight Star. Bloody hell.

I tell you nothing went right after they wrecked the Miner's Arms. I blame it all on that redevelopment company. I 'ope they go bust.

New Life

by Anna Newman

You have gone
And I remain
Alone
Abandoned
Stripped of the companionable life I knew
With you
Who are held so dear, so precious in my fragile heart.

You are no more
And I remain
Alone
Perplexed
Straining my ears to hear you in the silence of Not There
Willing my sore eyes to see you at every turn.

You are no more
And I remain
Alone,
Bewildered by the enormity of Death
Struck numb by the emptiness that once held you.

You are no more
And I remain
Alone, in solitude
Regarding a future that had no form,
No pathway,
No joy,
No love,
No you.

You are no more
But I am here

Alone, it's true
But, though beaten by the savagery of grief
I yet remain
Alive.

Alive in this world which once gave you such delight.
You loved the wild birds, which now I feed for you
You loved the deserted beaches and cliff paths
Which now I walk for you.
You loved the colours and textures of your artist's world
Which now I observe for you,
Borrowing your senses to make a less alien place for my survival.

You are no more
But I am here
Alive
Recalling your words once spoken in tenderness
And nestling them away in the soft places of my heart
Where they will live and heal.

You are no more
But I am
I hear you speak to me, whispering of new life.
I must learn again to exist alone in a world of couples
To shoulder myself the decisions and responsibilities of a solitary being.

You are no more in this world
But I must be
Your courage, your humour, your love
Live on through me.

Winter Comes

by Anna Newman

Winter comes as creeping death
Scything leaves from trees and
Laying bare the skeletons of summer gardens.

Winter comes like lethal sleep
To brave, late autumn flowers
That wither on their crippled stems

Winter comes as fearful darkness
Crushing a pale sun into
Low late rising and early setting
Begrudging the daylight hours.

Winter comes as liquid gold
Defusing limpid light over frosted fields
Bound by twiggy hedgerows and bared nests

Winter comes as freezing limbs
Frozen toes and red-nipped noses
With a cruel north wind like flying knives
Slicing and hacking the icy air.

Winter comes as sparkling fun
Snowmen, sledges, and hot buttered toast
Eaten around the dancing flames of
Warm log fires.
Winter comes as rest
A deep, cold breath
To put the world to sleep.

But winter comes as transformation
An alchemy of magic and miracle
An illusion of death, hiding new life

And guarding the precious flame
Of spring.

Winter Delights

by John Cliff

"Come Michael, let's go up to Burley Hill.
Last night's snowfall glistens in the field
All crisp and still.
Call for Frank, he's got a super sledge
With polished runners; it's fast but he can turn it
Before the hedge.
Mine is heavy the army used. David and Lin
Can share with me a long twisting glide
Navigating the deeper snow.
We shan't sink 'cause the runners are wide."

"Is that old 'Hodgy' and Chris off Eaton Bank?
See, trudging across from Flaxholme meadow.
(You know them, Frank,
We met them last year on Holbrook Moor
When you were acting stupid and fell off your bike.
They live next door
To grumpy-guts who bawled foul language at us
For crossing the weir to Peckwash Mill.).
Hey, 'Hodgy', Chris, come with us,
We're going sledging on Burley Hill."

A sledge train, like seven juvenile human ants
On iced-cake anthill, runner blades scribing lines,
Snow encrusted pants
Rolling on a blanket of winter sky.

Seeing two others come up from Quarndon side
Lin shouts "Hi!"
They each pull a sledge. Lin plods uphill
And talks awhile. She yells "It's Susan and Mark",
(She knows their house on Burley Lane
Rather posh by Allestree Park).

So nine of us take the hill, Chris thrusting a bough
Into the summit snow, my scarf flying the flag.
Upon the brow
We cheer and laugh the time away
As fresh snow falls to crown our conquest
This wintry day.
Soon tiring we shepherd in the sledges;
Now we are snowmen making plans: we borrow
Minutes from our childhood winter -
To make the hours of memories tomorrow.

Lines in a Wolverhampton Cemetery on a wet, grey Sunday Afternoon

by Anna Newman

Grey roofs on a wet Sunday
Misty chill, stretching into infinity
Steadily dripping rain from dark, sad trees.
Houses, row on row, all alike
Huddled and clustered up and down the glistening hills.
The living,
Trapped alive in their urban prisons.

The Cemetery
With verdigris crosses and weary-eyed angels,
Drooping flowers in dull brass bowls,
Mildewed headstones and lichened lettering
Fading in the moss
The dead
Trapped inert in their urban prisons.

Alive and dead
All trapped
Limited by birth, geography and
The blinkered parameters of parents' horizons
From the womb to the house to the grave
Confined in boxes all their lives.

Last Chance

by Anna Newman

It's his birthday today. We sit in the restaurant and I look at him over the rim of my wine glass. In the candlelight he is still handsome, with that easy, infectious smile and those oh, so sexy blue eyes.

I propose a toast to his thirty-nine years. He proposes a toast to our future. But our future is fragile. The past still crucifies me softly in the recesses of my heart. There have been too many infidelities, too many rows, too many betrayals…too many lies.

We can patch it all up, he says hopefully. I am not sure but I force myself to drain my glass. This is his last chance. He knows it.

He pays the bill and tips the waitress lavishly. She is young, with endless legs and long eyelashes. I try not to look. Instead I turn to the reception desk to pick up our coats. There is no-one there on duty, so I walk around the counter and retrieve my glittery shawl and his jacket.

It is not a long drive but we are tired. We go to the kitchen. I move aside the remains of his birthday cake and the sharp serrated knife that lies alongside. He goes to the bathroom, throwing his jacket onto the nearest chair. I put the coffee cups out on the work surface.

I turn and run one hand wearily over my forehead. I cannot erase the slow, throbbing headache nagging at me. Between my eyes.

As the coffee pot gurgles and hisses, I catch sight of his carelessly discarded jacket. A note. I see a folded note nearly falling out of the right pocket. With shaking fingers I unfold the paper – it is pink and perfumed.

The words are written with an extravagant, feminine hand. My sexy darling, it reads. I long for you so much. When can we meet again? I need you in my arms to kiss you, to love you. See if you can get her out of the way this weekend like you promised. All my love forever, Andrea.

My stomach lurches and I grip the note, giddy and sick with apprehension. The past – that awful mixture of anxiety, rage and jealousy rises like bile within me.

As he comes back through the door, I screw the note up violently, my nails cutting through the paper and into my palm.

'You bastard,' I scream. 'You bloody scheming bastard.'

He rocks back on his heels and averts his head as the love note hits his eyes.

'What are you on about?' he demands. 'What's this?' He bends down to pick it up.

'Sexy darling,' I shout, with a scorn that seems vomit from my mouth. 'Andrea?' I spit the name in his face. He blinks as he looks at the crumpled note.

'This isn't mine,' he exclaims. The bewilderment in his voice deserves an Oscar. 'Where'd you get it from?'

'Your bloody jacket. You've done it again, haven't you? Another silly little tart to join all the rest. All my life you've been unfaithful, time and time again,' I was screaming.

'Darling, I swear I don't know about this. You must believe me. We're going to make a new future together. I told you I've changed...no more affairs...I don't even know an Andrea.'

'Don't lie again,' I screamed. 'I've heard it all before...remember?'

I am crying hot, bitter tears now.

His face hardens and he comes towards me. 'Patty, listen. I don't know who wrote this. I've never seen it before. You must believe me.'

'Oh must I? Must I really? Well I don't. I don't believe you and I never will. Get out of here – now!'

He tries to take me in his arms. I wriggle and elbow him viciously. He holds me even tighter and whispers desperately in my ear.

'Patty, Patty, listen…listen to me…please. I swear on our children's lives that I know nothing about that note. I don't know how it got there. I've changed. I realise what a fool I've been. I told you I'd never do it again.'

'No,' my fury, my rage, my pent-up anger of twenty years suddenly sets into a cold resolve. I reach out with my free arm and my hand closes around the cake knife. 'No…you won't.'

He releases me, hope and relief lighting his face.

I take my chance. I harness all my strength and force the knife into his chest. I twist and turn the blade. I am screaming at him.

His face contorts as he staggers back – my name on his lips. Both his hands go to the knife handle, but he has already fallen against the door frame. He slumps down, gurgles as blood surges into his mouth and trickles down his chin. His eyes register disbelief. His hands rise in supplication and his chest heaves. Then he is still. The last echo of my screams fade. The silence closes in around me.

I cannot bear his eyes. They are still open, staring at me, accusing me. I take his jacket from the chair and fling it over his face from where I stand, shaking. It is when it lands that the wallet skids out of the inside pocket and falls into the expanding pool of blood. I stare at it. The horror I have covered up in his eyes is now mirrored in mine.

It is not his wallet…not his jacket.

Solstice

by John Cliff

The day does not dawn,
It merely shows itself
But briefly to pay homage
To a turn of tide and time,
While the sun takes refuge.

The last relics of Autumn
Are woven into a thicket
Of winter willow and ash
And the song of a rumbling river
Sings in sepia meadows.

Old life clings to the unborn
In the womb of season's sepulchre,
Sleeping in grey-veiled woods
Guarded by the ancestors
Of the earth-born spirit.

Daylight is fading, fusing
With the consummate darkness
In the valley of the night-bird :
The soaring messenger of hope
Carrying sacred mistletoe

Into the first dawn
Of rebirth; a different nativity
In nature's cradle.
Where earth-born spirit rises
In fertile woods …

And green meadows greet the rumbling river
And the solstice song is sung.

Bills Of Lading

by John Cliff

During the seventies,
Routinely at my desk
I would load my pipe with Three Nuns tobacco
And sort through the day's post.

'Attention Mr J Cliff, Export Department,'
One from the shipping company.
I examine the ornate crest on the envelope
As I strike a match and drew on the pipe.

Curls of blue smoke would gather in the motionless atmosphere.
The phone often rang,
My colleague answering and scrawling notes.
His pipe lying dormant beside an empty coffee stained mug
Bearing the name Ellerman Wilson Line.

I open the envelope.
'Dear Sir,
Please find enclosed Bills of Lading
As requested, etcetera, etcetera.'

I am fascinated by these documents,
They have a language of their own:
"In Witness whereof
The Master of this Vessel
Having affirmed to three
Bills of Lading
One of which being accomplished
The others to stand Void"

I once thought it would make a nice chant
A bit like a psalm.
It would have to end with an Amen.

I wonder what Bills of Lading look like today.
What do they say?
Have computers taken the magic away?
Are they turned out faster and faster
And witnessed whereof by any ship's master.?
And marine insurance, what does that say?
Whether cover is FPA
With different conditions for WA
Is CIF and FOB
Still used for exports sent by sea?

Lord, I pray it's just the same
Old familiar shipping game
As masters steer their vessels wide
From port to port on every tide.
With every charter well deployed
No Bill of Lading shall stand void.

Amen.

Poppycock & Humbug
(a canine encounter with the henhouse brigade)
by John Cliff

It was Christmas with everything hunky-dory in the household of Freddy and Poppy and mistress Annabel Bluemer. Freddy was a well-bred Labrador cross exercising his responsibilities in a deep sleep. Poppy, a dog-like creature called a greyhound decided to go for one of her routine patrols of the garden. Putting her long nose into anything and everything that might produce edible results she disturbed something in the frosted foliage by the pond. Her brain engaged gear. She pushed her snout rapidly through the reeds. A frog would do nicely. But it was not a frog that bit her on the nose. She retreated yelping and spitting.

"Serves you right," came a low-pitched squeaky voice.

"Mm?" muttered Poppy.

"Pushing your ugly nose into my patch, you half-baked streak."

"Mm?" repeated a confused dog whose brain was having difficulty re-engaging.

A rodent of ample proportion emerged from cover. It eye-balled Poppy. Poppy eye-balled back. It had a large silver streak on its head.

"Listen, brainless, I'm in charge here, so watch where you're snooping, eh!"

"Snooping!" snapped Poppy. Then as her brain found gear again, "What a nice meal you are."

"Don't get ideas or it'll be worse for you. You're speaking to Rodentius, commander of the henhouse rat brigade. I'm in charge of the toughest well-drilled force in the neighbourhood. And don't forget it."

"Rodentius!" exclaimed Poppy with a snitter. "What a funny name."

"Quiet you moth-eaten dog. I'm important and well respected. I know humans are celebrating something called Christmas at this time of year and there's a mountain of good food being chucked out for us rats to have a feast. We don't intend to share it with ugly canines either. I think I'm like what they call Father Christmas, What's your name?"

"Poppy," came the reply.

"Poppycock, I'd call you." Rodentius pondered for a moment. "You could be a mascot at our favourite watering hole, the Poppycock & Humbug".

"What's that?" asked Poppy

"A pub– at the other end of the sewer. Sawdust and spit, pork scratchings and stale beer. Paradise."

Poppy was enthused. "I like stout. I like the brandy what mistress gave me for a good night's sleep. Said it was for her to sleep, though. Anyway, I drank it.

"You got taste, then, scrawny legs."

"I'll have you know I've got a pedigree as well."

"Oh, yeah, and what's one of those?"

Poppy thought for a very brief moment, which was quite a long time for her.

"My mistress said it's written in my ear. That's right, a sort of code."

"Impressive, whatever it is. Seems like I could make some use of you. What you good at?"

"Killing," came a quick response.

"What! I could be impressed. "Hey, gang, here a minute."

Then from nowhere appeared a number of smaller rats encircling Rodentius and Poppy. They were chattering excitedly in small voices, viewing the large greyhound before them with caution.

"Okay boys," said the big rat. "Meet Poppy - er - Poppycock the killer canine."

The brigade responded to the announcement with 'oooh's' and 'aaah's' and a volley of chatter.

"Pull yourselves together. ATTEN.....SHUN!" ordered Rodentius.

The other rats tried to contain themselves as they fell back into line.

Poppy had by now developed a curiosity which surprisingly surpassed her appetite for a rodent feast. She couldn't fathom what was going on. Her brain told her that rats don't speak dog language yet there she was conversing with them. Was it the turkey mistress Annabel had fed her in the morning or the brandy last night? Was Freddy responsible? Were they out to get her? Was it a conspiracy? Poppy was overstretching her brain and it was tiring. She felt like running away. And her nose hurt. It was also dripping in the cold.

"I wanna lie down a bit," whinged Poppy.

"Lie down, do you. Oh no, not yet, you lanky streak. I've got to introduce you to the gang, then talk about plans - big plans. You could make a name for yourself. Yeah, and be a real mascot."

The group started to giggle with excitement

"Right, pay attention." Rodentius stood on his back legs and pointed out the other rats by name. Poppy wondered how he did that without falling over as the other rats squeaked their names: Pinkerton, Benji, Nando, Strider, Pocksy, Regent, Leaf mould.

"Leaf mould?" enquired Poppy.

"That's right. Best disguise in the business."

"Can I lie down?" Poppy put on her best whinge which never failed to grab attention.

"Oh if you must. I'll be back later with plans. Big plans. Dream about fame you toothy ragbag."

The tribe melted into the background as Poppy went through the tedious motions of lying down, not easy when you've got overstretched legs affixed to a long body and icy ground underneath. She thought as best she could about the situation. She can't tell Freddy. If he believed her the whole dog world would know. 'Heck, I could spew thinking about it,' she said to herself, before coughing audibly, a rather unpleasant habit she had perfected. Then her brain focussed with unusual clarity. Maybe this Rodentius can get me away. Yes, that's it. I'll be a great leader of rats. Did he say the henhouse rat brigade. Hens. HENS. Oh, don't I just love 'em.' She rolled over on the garden path, snittered and fell asleep.

"Wake up you ugly joint." Rodentius had come back with one of his 'boys'.

Poppy lifted her head, yawned and grunted at the same time.

"Oh it's you."

"Me and Strider the Invincible. Let's get down to business. That is when you can raise yourself."

Poppy half sat up, coughed and grimaced. "Fine. I'm all ears."

Rodentius looked about him menacingly, his silver streak raised like a crown. " And you're going to need 'em. The pigeon loft gang has been scouting and..."

"Pigeons!" interrupted Poppy

"Shut it, goofy. As I was saying, the scouts overheard the tip gang boasting about a take-over of our row." Rodentius faced Poppy at close range. "We and the pigeon lofters have lived together for a very long time and we ain't partial to a take-over, right!. The tip gang are notorious big guys. Boy, you don't know how big. Raw muscle from living on rich garbage, razor sharp teeth from chewing bed frames and fridges And we aint sharing our pickings. They spell trouble. We need strength and speed to match and YOU claim to be a killer. Yeah, a killing machine like what you are could be our salvage."

"Salvation," corrected Strider.

"What about it? You've got the teeth," Rodentius eye-balled Poppy and whispered softly in her ear: "A streamlined serpent like you could make mincemeat of those bloated bullies. You'd have your own command of the best from the henhouse and pigeon loft gangs ....AND a reward for success is a fat juicy chicken and a fat juicy pigeon, every day, washed down with anything you fancy at the Poppycock and Humbug." Humans call it Christmas and I can promise you Christmas every day."

"Yes, yes, no problem Rodentius, sir, I'm ready when you are." Poppy could hardly contain herself, panting with anticipation.

"Those teeth are a sure winner," observed Strider. "I'm going to give you a run-down of our finest tuned, stealth trained , tactical expert rats as you could wish for. They're mean looking just like you."

Poppy agreed. " Yeah, I'm feeling real mean and a fraction hungry."

Everything was moving fast, real fast, and Poppy was dizzy with excitement. They had moved to the bottom corner of the garden in a hollow behind the shrubs where holes under the fence gave the rats access to and from the henhouse. Strider had Poppy's fighting team at the ready. She had never before seen such a mean looking array of front teeth flashing before her.

Rodentius started. "Listen, lanky-legs, we're going to dig you out but you'll have to help. We've got a passage started, see, at the back here. Now get them feet working."

"Wow," enthused Poppy as she began scraping and kicking.

"News is the tip gang have sent a posse already."

"A posse?" queried Poppy. "Can I kill it?"

"Kill it, eat it, spit it out. All yours, pea-brain."

Poppy felt she was under a spell. But what a spell. She didn't care as long as there was a kill and a feast at the end. 'And endless chickens and pigeons. Dog heaven,' she thought. 'And maybe tip rats are edible.' She knew, strangely, that the rats of the henhouse and pigeon loft brigades were untouchable. The spell or whatever it was had that effect. Well, she was nearly one of them by now.

There was a sudden commotion beyond the fence. "Great steaming sewers, they're here." Rodentius and a multitude of rats were scurrying everywhere. "Take up positions," he shouted. "You, alligator hound, get at 'em. They're coming up to the pigeon lofters. We'll cut 'em off at the rear. Go, go, go!"

Poppy blindly leapt into new territory. And leapt…and leapt…and felt herself being pulled down and down. Her senses were distorted. She could hardly breathe. Gigantic rats were running all over her, getting bigger, heavier. She bared her teeth, snapping, kicking her legs as hard as she could. She heard screams, saw pigeons and hens and rats flying in empty space, going round and round in circles. Her brain was doing the same in much smaller circles. Nothing was clear any more. 'Rodentius!' she choked, but the only sound was a splutter. 'Strider!' Names were spiriting away as were pigeons and hens and rats, yet she was spluttering, spitting and hearing new sounds, and there was mistress Annabel.

'Mistress Annabel!'

"Bloody Poppy get out of that pond right now, you sod. What are you doing in there."

Poppy emerged from the icy shallow water very confused.

"I thought you were up to something when Freddy came in. What's that you've got there? A pigeon! YOU - GET IN THAT HOUSE!

Poppy stared blankly at the paving. Indeed there was a dead pigeon. She shook herself. She couldn't make sense of anything. Freddy was sitting there looking important with a big smirk on his face. Poppy choked and hacked, feeling too sick to add a whinge. Grudgingly she waddled up the garden path then stopped momentarily in her tracks. She was conscious of a low-pitched squeaky voice whispering faintly in her ear. "Well done, Major Poppycock..........well............done."

Later, as Poppy lay sulking, Mistress Annabel Bluemer went down the garden to remove the pigeon. She also found a dead rat with a strange silver streak on its head.

Father Humbug

by Anna Newman

At just five years old I was a worried child. I was worried about Father Christmas.

Thus far, I had accepted he arrived on a sleigh pulled by reindeer, parked on the roof, and came down the chimney with my presents. Simple. Except one day, I started wondering about how. After a couple of days of hard pondering, I needed answers.

My mum was the first port of call. How did Father Christmas get down the chimney? Why didn't his sleigh and the reindeer slip off the roof? Did he tie them to the chimney pot? What if the chimney pot broke off? How many presents did he carry at one time? How did he know who lived where? What if there were no chimneys, like if I was an African child who lived in a mud hut? How come he didn't get all sooty? How did he actually get down the chimney, because when the sweep came last he couldn't get his brush through at one point? Well, only after a lot of pushing, panting and swearing. Did Father Christmas swear? What language did he speak? Anyway, how did he afford all those presents? Where did he get the money from? What if he got stuck in the chimney and couldn't move? We couldn't light the fire then, and we would get cold and the house would freeze up and that reminded me that igloos only had one hole to get through and it wasn't in the roof and the reindeer might…

Wearily Mum stemmed the tide of words. Magic, she said. It's all done by magic. Special magic.

She returned to her knitting. I digested this news carefully, and for a day or so was happy with it. Then it occurred to me. 'Mum,' I said. 'You know Father Christmas gets down the chimney by magic?'

'Yes,' said Mum, probably with some foreboding.

'Well,' I continued. 'Why doesn't he get in somewhere else by magic, like doors and windows? Why the chimney? Anyway, it would be better for the reindeer to land on the lawn properly…then they couldn't slide down the roof tiles.'

'I don't know,' said Mum weakly. 'He could get in anywhere if he chose. Just happens to favour chimneys.'

I went away to think again. So…he could get in anywhere he liked? Hmmm…for the next day or so I imagined him coming through every opening in the house. Going to the toilet became a nightmare. At any moment he could slip in the door or window and catch me on the toilet seat with my knickers round my ankles. Oh dear!

And then, as children do, I got a fixation. I had always been nervous of the little gap you get between curtains at the top, when you pull them together. I became convince that he would suddenly catapult into the room through that gap when I least expected him.

I probably made my parents' lives a misery from then on. In the end Mum couldn't stand my sobs and my nervous twitches any longer.

'For goodness sake, George, you tell her,' she said to Dad.

Poor Dad, he always got the rotten jobs.

'He won't come in anywhere,' said Dad. 'He isn't true.'

'But,' I said. 'Who gives me my presents then?'

'We do,' said Dad.

'What about Auntie Glad's presents?'

'She doesn't give them to Father Christmas,' said Dad. 'She gives them to us and we put them at the bottom of your bed in a pillowcase when you're asleep. Which is where I wish you were now,' he added morosely.

'Oh, so he won't come in through the curtains?' I asked.

Well, what a relief. From then on I was quite happy that Father Christmas did not exist. It made believing in him so easy – I could now believe with renewed vigour and confidence because he simply wasn't there.

I suspect there's an analogy with religion here…but I didn't know that then.

A Christmas Journey

by John Cliff

I was standing on the brink of a dream
Waiting to fall,
When the sky took me away
Into starlight of another Time,
And I saw in youthful spirit
A December evening long ago.
There, in dreamlike haze, Christmas lights
Mimicked the stars.
I was flying
Yet motionless on Wings of Time
In a grey mist of dust,
And a child's hand grasped at the starlight
As it expired
In the Ashes of Time.

Suddenly I found a star
Glowing, growing in my hand
Consuming me with its radiance
As I was borne to a place
Where Christmas lights were swaying, unlit
In a dark and empty street.
Then my star set them aglow
Into a pageant of colour and warmth,
Drawing people from their houses,
Gathering beneath the brightness
Singing carols
As the grey mist of dust became snow flakes
Falling, falling from a sky which took me
From the brink of a dream
Into a four year old's Christmas.
Spellbound, I stepped from the Wings of Time
To sweep snow from a window ledge;
Peering, on tiptoe, through the pane
I saw a tree festooned with garlands,
And heard the music of laughter
As I found myself inside familiar walls.
There was my little bed.
I was dreaming
Within a dream of memories
Watching the old heater glowing,
Its faint smell of paraffin
Soothing to my nostrils.
But I knew I must go to sleep
Before he came with the presents,
While the snow outside became my starlit blanket within.
Then I roused from nostalgic slumber
Daring to peek over the sheets

To see the bulging pillowcase *he* had left.
A clockwork train set, I remember,
Crayons, a drawing book, too.
The living room fire flickered and crackled
As my train orbited the wrapping paper.
The goose was in the oven
Before they came round from next door.
Merry Christmas!
Merry Christmas!
But the greeting faded into an empty echo
And I couldn't stay.
Goodbye youthful spirit,
I must journey once more
On the Wings of Time,
Flying, flying,
Yet motionless
In a grey mist of dust
Swirling in a cold wind, sliced by a naked tree
Bowing in prayer over a grave
In the Ashes of Time.
I hear the wind in the trees
Like old familiar voices
Which I cannot make out,
Yet know in that darkness
There is a message.
I open a hand
Of more than three score years
And in its palm find my star
Glowing, growing,
Washing me in its radiant tide,
Ebbing from the brink of a dream
On Christmas Eve.

The Christmas Stable Scene

by Anna Newman

This is a true story that happened when I was four years old and which produced, in the end, a valuable lesson. Although I did not quite see it that way at the time.

That Christmas Mum bought me a plastic, made in China, Christmas Stable Scene. My Dad would have had nothing to do with this purchase, because he often used to say how could there be a God with so much suffering in the world?

Many years later I sort of knew what he meant, but in the meantime I opened my little package and found a TREASURE!

In case you're thinking at this point, 'poor little mite' with only a cheap plastic Nativity scene for Christmas, I must add to that a Rupert Annual and a Triang scooter, so I really did quite well that year.

Anyway, there it was – a brown plastic triangle, about three inches high and two and a half at the base. It had a severe wobble but a bit of plasticine soon cured that. There was a crudely painted blue Mary, a garish purple Joseph, a violent orange cow and, for some unfathomable reason, a green sheep! In the centre in a manger lay a featureless baby Jesus, which had at least the requisite number of arms and legs and those, more or less, in the right places. The orange cow was sadly afflicted with five legs. Mary and Joseph's nether regions were fortunately never formed under their robes. Who knows what they may have been like…?

But I was enchanted. I sat it in front of me on the dining room table and re-enacted the Christmas story, reciting all the parts over and over again as only children can. I dressed up some wooden clothes pegs in rags for the shepherds and in scraps of velvet for the three kings. The fact that they were taller than the stable itself did not bother me. I had imagination on my side. I do remember that after a while Mum closed the kitchen door meaningfully. No doubt I was on my ninth recital by them.

After Christmas the precious stable scene sat on my bedroom window sill all year. Every night I knelt in front of it to say my prayers. This tended to take a long time, even at the age of four, because I was developing a 'conscience'. After calling down blessing on my Mum, my Dad, my Gran, Lucky the budgie, and Panda the cat – and all my friends and enemies – I felt duty bound to include my wider family. Even Auntie Gladys, who had sent me a pair of ghastly pink coat hangers for which I was extremely ungrateful. But before I could get off my knees, I had to remember all the people and animals in our universe who were sick, old or poor, or all those things. I was anxious to get this right in case God should leave anybody out. I clearly did not trust Him even then!

The year passed and soon the next Christmas loomed. My prayer ritual in front of the stable scene had become an absolute necessity before I could go to sleep. And it was getting longer… and longer… and longer. As it lengthened I grew increasingly more tired and had to think of a way of saving myself, never mind the rest of the world.

The stable scene was the problem. As long as it was there I felt bound to do the prayer ritual. But what if it wasn't there? Ah, then I would be free to cut short my prayers to a simple God-bless-everything-that-is-alive and not alive in the whole universe and any more universes He might have made and not mentioned.

It was then that the Grand Idea presented itself in my mind, like a miracle. I would give the crib away! But not just to anybody. No, no, I would give it to God to pass on to Baby Jesus. He would love this splendid present.

I was, by then, just under five and couldn't conceive that God would fail to take it and give it to Baby Jesus. After all, Mum was always saying God could do anything. My Dad countered this by saying he wasn't choosing to do much good then, was he. But Mum took no notice of that blasphemy.

On Christmas Eve, in addition to the interminable prayers, which I hoped I was uttering for the last time, I triumphantly gave the stable scene to God. I just knew for a fact that it would be gone by Christmas Morning.

When I drew back the curtains on December 25th I was, for once, struck dumb; it was still there. This simply could not be. I yanked the curtains back and forth experimentally, but no – it remained in garish splendour on the window sill.

All through the day I tried to make sense of this. Perhaps God would take it after breakfast? No. Perhaps after Christmas Dinner? No. I was a bit hazy about God's domestic arrangements, and not sure who would cook His dinner. Maybe I should have offered a slice of turkey instead? Come the afternoon I was aggrieved, and by bedtime I was furious. It had always been drilled into me that gifts should be received with good grace, even if you hated them as much as I hated Aunt Glad's coat hangers, which I had thrown into the back of the wardrobe. Mum had made me write a thank you letter to Aunt Glad even though I was deeply resentful.

Now I was beginning to realise how my aunt would have felt if I had rejected her gift as rudely as God had rejected mine. Could God be that bad mannered? Or worse, could God not care?

That night I cried myself to sleep with angry tears. I forgot to pray. In the morning I decided it served God right that I hadn't reminded Him of His duty to creation.

That plastic stable lived on for many years on my window sill. Gradually bits fell off and got lost. But I still have the green sheep in Mum's button box. On reflection, I gleaned a worthwhile lesson from my cheap plastic stable that all gifts should be received with gratitude and sensitivity and the giver's feelings should never, ever be hurt.

Foggy Reflections on Life Old and New

from the diary letters of John Cliff

14th January

A hard overnight frost had our village tightly in its grip when daylight came. It was not one of those bright, crisp mornings when everything about sparkles in winter sunshine; more exactly it was a sombre grey and depressing scene through the open window blinds. A fog had descended with the frost and I was decidedly comfortable staying indoors.

Later the shroud lifted slightly but the day refused to let in the sunshine. As one needs sustenance at some point beyond breakfast, and the food cupboard would shortly resemble that of Old Mother Hubbard, a walk to the shop was advisable. When I stepped out the frost had all but gone. The moisture laden air was cold, dripping from the trees along the driveway to the lane. It is surprising how one bucks up once the air hits the lungs and the arms and legs get moving.

On my way I passed through the churchyard which is a pleasant diversion from the main road. Pleasant, I would add, only with respect to the overall aspect and serenity one observes among the resting places of the departed. Quite often when I walk this way I stop to read inscriptions on headstones and wonder what sort of life the deceased had lived. A profusion of new graves are lining the well-tended grassy earth which is a little alarming since, not so long ago, there didn't seem anywhere near as many. One has to be philosophical and assume the older inhabitants have been called in by their maker in quick succession for the sake of expediency. Conversely, one sometimes contemplates the injustices of life when observing a stone into which is etched a colourful 'Postman Pat' and bearing an epitaph to a little girl buried at the tender age of four and a half.

Returning down the lane with a shopping bag full of edible goodies I was met by a lively little chap in the hedgerow. A great tit followed me all the way to the bottom, pronouncing his presence with that familiar metallic chirp and bouncing from one bare twig to another to keep up with me. I hope to meet him again. There is a sense of expectation in this wintry atmosphere. Above me, as I turned from the lane, a few rooks were holding a meeting way up in the tree branches, inspecting the old nests and probably discussing mortgage dilemmas and the raising of families. It sounded as though they were having one or two disagreements.

Life goes on.

Catering in the Winter Kitchen

from the diary letters of John Cliff

4th February

This week has thrown winter at us, just as I was thinking that spring could be creeping upon us before long. A few inches of snow over a couple of days put paid to hopes of a sudden awakening of a new season.

Today the car stayed in the driveway, which was not a bad thing because the idea of a vigorous walk up the snowbound lane to the village shop was rather appealing as well as being good for the constitution. I had already decided to dabble in culinary matters and required an item or two to throw into a selected recipe, anticipating the finished creation would resemble the wonderful mouth watering picture in the recipe book.

The lane was unexpectedly clear apart from the verges. Someone must have chivvied the local council to inform them of its existence. We've been waiting for it to be resurfaced so I'm told for goodness knows how many years. The road repair men always appear occupied digging holes in somebody else's road when they would be better employed filling existing holes in ours. Anyway I digress, for I must say that the hedgerows and fields looked magnificent in their mantle of white. A blackbird was busily shuffling around the hedge bottom, turning up old leaves for any tasty morsel he could find. He stopped momentarily to give me a stare then diligently resumed his search in nature's winter kitchen. One is inclined to smile at some creatures' antics foraging for food in the snow; to us an amusing sight but to them a matter of survival.

I have to say how comforting it was to be back from the shop and inside where it was nice and warm. The kettle was soon humming and I was spreading out ingredients for a session of Masterchef with the recipe page propped up on the worktop. Once the tea had brewed I was supping a mugful while reading the baking procedures for the umpteenth time. One who aspires to the dizzy heights of gastronomic excellence can't be too careful. For this delight, a savoury tart, I had to roll out puff pastry to line a flan tin. The block of pastry was rectangular which posed a problem since the tin was round. Undaunted, I exercised great skill in reproducing a rough circle of dough to fit, the result being quite pleasing if not exhausting. The kitchen became a nucleus of throbbing activity: oven on, chopped ingredients sizzling in a pan on the stove, eggs cracked and stirred with cream. My kitchen is modest but the mileage I cover on these occasions is not inconsiderable. There is always an essential utensil I had forgotten about which is right at the back of the cupboard, then I have to stir something on the cooker behind me, or sieve or blend on the worktop in front, each stage generating an incredible stack of washing-up to be piled haphazardly by the sink.

However, one's efforts are not in vain when the time comes to remove a perfectly baked tart from the oven and gloat over one's expertise in creative cuisine. One should avoid making a comparison with an illustration, which no doubt has been subjected to professional photo conjuring. Instead, just savour with due modesty one's adeptness before savouring the flan.

The Winter Hearth

by John Cliff

There's something nostalgic about a real coal fire in a real fireplace in wintertime. Watching from the hearth as a child the first cold flames devouring newspaper and lapping the kindling sticks. Dad strategically placing small coals over the sticks, or sometimes firelighters. Slowly the flames took hold and warmth began to filter from the grate, announced by crackling and spitting. The brassy coal bucket was filled from the outside shed or bunker, occasionally arriving at the hearth with an icing of snow which would add a musical hiss to the growing flames. In blizzard conditions snow was driven through gaps in the coal store where it lay in thin white streaks. Our coal arrived on the backs of strong men in leather aprons, usually two of them who tipped with apparent ease Hessian sacks one after another, the contents thundering into the shed. Then a black-faced man would produce a grubby piece of paper, scrawl on it and pass it to Dad for payment. Some pieces of coal were enormous and had to be broken up with a heavy hammer. Often they would be shiny and splinters like black icicles would fall away.

The coldest winter evenings were occasions to sit around the fireplace and listen to the radio: The Goon Show, Hancock, or for me Dan Dare, Pilot of the Future. Television didn't arrive at our house until the Coronation. I used to be hypnotised by the fire, drawn into a fantasy world where brave explorations happened, mighty chasms crossed, explosive flames dodged and eruptions of boiling ooze avoided. That was the tar bubbling from hot coals. There was always a way through , dangerous but possible leaps across steaming cauldrons, scrambles along the cooler edges of dark, foreboding rocks overlooking a white hot morass in the very bowels of the furnace. One slip would mean instant evaporation. Intrepid as the imaginary explorers were, other dangers lurked in the hot caverns: dragons unseen within their lairs shooting orange and white forked tongues unexpectedly around and through gaps, threatening escape routes: landslips caused by movements in the underlying morass as volcanic material dropped into the ash pan. At any moment it could be necessary for these most skilful and experienced explorers to take immediate evasive action to ensure survival. I was one of them.

Eventually the fire had to be 'made up,' a job even I was allowed to do. That would be the end of an episode. Soon another scene would emerge and the hearth would be alive with adventure again, often dangerous, always successful. The fireplace itself was of plain buff or green tiles, art deco style, on top of which stood a mantle clock and Dad's pipe rack. He possessed two or three pipes, with pipe cleaners kept nearby in a narrow pot on the shelf. He smoked Three Nuns tobacco, at times a Balkan Sobranie which I was told smelt like camel dung, the aroma hanging around for ages. I don't think we had air fresheners then, although the smell was not as bad as it sounded. Smoke was particularly prevalent around Christmas when Dad received a tin of tobacco and a packet of cigars from Santa Claus.

Dad's pipe was no contest for gusts of wind which sometimes blew down the chimney sending sooty palls of smoke into the living room. It meant Mum had to get out the duster and wipe around the affected areas, mostly the hearth, mantle shelf and sideboard. The Hoover would come out tomorrow.

Those days are long gone, of course. The last open fire I had, many years on from childhood dreams, was in the eighties. The surround was an old tiled sort, not dissimilar to the one from thirty odd years before. I took it out and built a stone one, yet the fire in the grate didn't change all that much. Neither did the delivery men in leather aprons heaving the sacks into the coal place, tendering sooty bills against which I paid far more than my parents ever did. The snows came and went. Cold nights outside were warm ones around the winter hearth and I do believe I saw the makings of another great adventure in the infant flames.

Equinox

by John Cliff

"Oh this cannot be right," said Thor
From his cave on pinnacled rock;
"'Tis turn of season , I've opened the door,
I want to make thunder
To crack clouds asunder,
To waken the nymphs, what's more.

"What do I see in the valley below,
Who dares to freeze my abode,
I blame that queen of winter snow;
There is no reason
To extend her season.
That ice witch will have to go."

"Be silent you noisy brutish thing,"
Commanded the winter queen.
"My snowbird has a sweet song to sing;
A lullaby to ice
Is far too nice
To be spoilt by the thought of spring."

"I am not a thing, I am a god
For heaven's sake," boomed Thor.
"At equinox my golden rod
Opens up the skies
Which, your majesty, implies
It's time to turn the earthy sod.

"And another thing before you leave,
Unless you decide to melt,
The valley is mine, see the river weave
Round crags and trees,
I have all these -

And water-nymphs would you believe."

"Nymphs, and where are they I pray?"
(The queen was not amused)
"Ah," exclaimed Thor, "not here today,
But in the morning
As day is dawning
When snow and ice have gone away.

"The roof shall lift on winter sky
As I announce - with thunder -
Spring is here; the reason why
You should now go
And take your snow."
"Oh, huff," was all the queen did reply.

There came a soft voice from an old holly tree.
The winter king had aroused:
"What are you doing my dear," said he,
"Cavorting with Thor?
That uncouth bore,
When you should be leaving with me.

"Harken to me for I know what's best,
We cannot stay any longer.
Our season has passed and our spirit must rest;
Late is the day,
We must be away,
The last winter sun hangs low in the west."

"Ha, ha," roared Thor from his pinnacled rock,
His golden staff raised up high.
"Tomorrow's sunrise will turn the clock,
And the goddess bring
The virgin spring,
And a verdant key to the valley unlock."

Thor slept well in his cave that night
As a storm washed winter away.
The morning awoke in an amber light
By the Manifold river where trout did play.
Water-nymphs bathed where the bright pools shone
As the goddess of spring stood on high.
Thor bowed out, his tempest gone,
He took his staff and bade goodbye.
"I shall return with the clock at the solstice hour,
Hold sway once more in my lofty lair,
When summer storms will heed my power;
Now you command this season fair."
The goddess cast her magic on every living thing
And her wisdom was the spell on the first rite of spring.

Miss Minton's Welcome

by Anna Newman

The house was derelict. I stood uncertainly on a scuffling of newspapers inside the door, trying to get my bearings in the dimness of sad, undrawn curtains and the grime of neglect.

'I'm sorry about the state of it,' the man said. Only my fiancée never really settled here. She moved in with me some years ago. She had central heating put in, though only used it once or twice.' He shivered, 'Tell you what, I'll try to get it going shall I?'

He skirted round the piles of rubbish and opened a door in the corner near the fireplace. As his footsteps thumped up the steep staircase I moved around carefully, getting a feel of the old building, once a home now a wreck.

Somehow, I thought, the house looked like I felt, down on its luck, lonely, and empty. I could sympathise. My husband had gone, our house sold, and this was all I could afford with my share of the pickings. I'd got half the money and both the dogs.

Some muffled noises on the landing told me the man had managed to switch on the boiler. I crossed to the radiator under the window and, with gloved fingers, tried to feel for the heat. By the time the man had come downstairs again I could sense a creeping warmth. It didn't reach my soul.

'All working,' he said with an anxious cheerfulness. He glanced at my face for a reaction. I smiled. I hadn't smiled for months and my mouth felt odd. I needed more practice.

He led me into the kitchen, dirty and dark. The lean-to roof had collapsed and weeds grew inside the house. There was a bathroom, grimy of course. For some reason the walls and ceiling were painted in a muddy turquoise colour. I didn't look inside the toilet pan. The lid was down. It could wait for rubber gloves and bleach. I pictured myself there on my knees, hair scooped out of the way, dissolving the filth of years. It was an oddly satisfying vision. More pictures skittered through my mind – scouring, cleaning, scrubbing, mending. Ah, but I hadn't said I would buy yet.

As we climbed the stairs, on hands and knees for the last four steps, so steep was the gradient, I experienced a sudden feeling of rightness. In the space of a heartbeat, I could see myself living here, could see myself making it bright, shining, warm and homely. I felt sorry for the house, not a vague sympathy but an overwhelming empathy. The house and I felt exactly the same, we were both unwanted.

By the time we had inspected the bedrooms, returned downstairs and emerged into the garden, I had made up my mind: I could love this house. I could make it proud again, for there were signs in the faded prettiness of the bedroom wallpaper, and here in the abandoned wilderness of the garden, that it had once been loved.

The man didn't sense my decision. He apologised for everything, especially the garden. That it was long and narrow. He couldn't know that of all things the garden would worry me least. He tried to point out possibilities but I was ahead of him. The courtyard, the Victorian shed, falling down like the house, the old Grecian statue by an overgrown pond. The patio, almost hidden by weeds – and the chestnut tree with wayward branches sweeping the ground. It had a wild, secret sweetness that promised my soul some peace at last.

Perhaps I could be reborn along with the house? I looked up at the outside, grey-grimed and crumbling. But would it want me? Would it welcome me, or would it reject me? It was only a glimmer of a thought, not one to share with him. When I said I would buy it as shown, he blinked stunned eyes. There was something else, he said, and that he should in all fairness tell me.

'Fact is,' he said. 'You might hear it has a bit of a reputation, noises and that. No-one seems to stay here for long…' he floundered. I could never bear people to be at a loss so I smiled again.

'No-one ever seems to stay with me for long either,' I replied.

The possibility of rats had not occurred to me until I crept onto my camp bed and closed my eyes. I had moved in that day, three months after my decision to buy. The dogs and I had set up our base in the tiny back bedroom, which had the distinction of being empty and relatively clean. I had not inspected the corners too closely.

My boxes and bits of furniture filled up the other rooms. I had no intention of unpacking until I had cleaned up the rubbish and dirt.

Why now? I thought. Why now when all I wanted was the oblivion of sleep, did my mind choose to imagine rats? I turned onto my back, tense with annoyance. Common sense told me the dogs were a sure defence and they were sleeping quietly alongside me.

Of course, once the rat idea had penetrated my tired brain, I could not be rid of it. Look, I told myself, there probably are rats. Rats go with derelict old houses: fact. Anyway, the dogs would hear them, would sense them long before I could. For goodness sake go to sleep I thought.

Two minutes later I was sitting bolt upright, my back against the wall. Sleep had retreated and I was now in the land of overtiredness. My mind would not stop thinking. I stared into the darkness and switched on the bedside light I strained my ears for the faint scratching of creatures, or the echoes of the past that old houses have trapped inside them. I looked at the dogs. They never stirred. Not even my demon mind could summon up the noises the man had talked about.

I picked up the book I was currently reading and attempted to enter another world for a time. Hopefully I would fall asleep, with the book falling on my face, waking me long enough to switch off the light. But not this time: I was wide awake. Eventually I heard the clock chime. Two strikes, two o'clock. Should I get up and make a cup of tea? Perhaps have a slice of toast? And then, naturally I wanted to go to the bathroom. I sighed with exasperation and not a little apprehension. I didn't really want to walk through the house alone in the dead of night. But finally I crawled out of the duvet and past the dogs, who turned onto their backs with their legs in the air – total enviable relaxation.

I negotiated the stairs, the living room, the kitchen and the bathroom, glad I had tipped half a bottle of bleach down the pan earlier. I tried hard not to think of rats coming up the plumbing and round the S-bend.

Back to the camp bed. I sat there and replayed the day in my mind. I could write about it in my diary I supposed. I scribbled for some time in the tiny pool of light in the tiny back bedroom of the tiny house that was now all mine. Three o'clock chimed distinctly. I sighed. My finger was dented from writing. I always gripped the pen so hard. I tried my book again, couldn't concentrate. I listened intently, no rats, not mysterious scratching and scurrying. I had rendered myself into this waking stating for nothing.

Four o'clock. The chimes rang out with old-fashioned sweetness through the still house. I tried to relax my body if not my mind. Quite suddenly I felt a strange gripping fear inch up my spine. With absolute horror I realised something oddly important…I had no chiming clock!

I remained in bed until morning, not sleeping at all. I lay there and listened with a paralysing intensity for the chimes at five o'clock. There were none. Six o'clock? Just silence in the house, although the dawn chorus was sweetening outside.

Some weeks later I was working in the garden, digging into the rich soil. The day was warm. I had discarded my scarf, then my jacket, hooking them on the lowest branch of the ancient damson tree. Once or twice I paused and stood straight to flex my back in the sunshine. The house, my house, looked happy I thought. We were comfortable together I fancied. I had indeed scrubbed and cleaned inside, just as I had imagined I would. My furniture and belongings had looked strange at first, awkward and self-conscious in their new surroundings. But as I worked on the house, and it began to look brighter, so my own raw feelings healed slightly.

I resumed my digging with energy when the spade struck something solid in the soil. I bent down' scrabbled the earth on the upturned spade and there, in tarnished glory, was a curved piece of china, crazed with age.

Once the dirt had been rubbed off it I could make out the colours, rose and soft green. The scrap was bumpy at one end, and more rubbing revealed half of what had once been some sort of cherub, winged and fat.

'Found any treasure then?' The voice of my elderly neighbour startled me.

'Yes,' I said and smiled. Smiles came more easily now. I held the fragment out for him to inspect over the fence. He took it from me, turned it this way and that in his rough old hands.

'Well I'll be blowed,' he exclaimed. 'I never thought to see this again.'

'What? What is it? What d'you mean.' 'I sounded impatient I knew.

'I do believe,' he pondered. 'That there piece of china was once part of Emily's clock. What a surprise after all these years.'

'Who was old Emily?'

'Miss Emily Minton?' Why, she were here long ago, when I were a lad. Old Emily had that there house of yourn back then. She were a character, and no mistake. Bit of a witch, some said, though she were always kind enough to me.'

'And that's part of a clock of hers?' I asked.

'That's right. Curious old thing it was, even then. Beautiful mind, but odd. Miss Emily had it for years she did, on the mantelpiece in the living room. Covered in roses it was, with a couple of them cherubby things either side.'

'Why was it odd?'

'Well, on account of its chime,' said the old man. He stopped. He had seen my sudden frown.

'Go on,' I prompted.

'Miss Emily's clock worked a treat,' he said. 'Ticked away perfectly and chimed the hours as sweet as a nut. But not when her nephew came. It stopped then right enough…'

'Why? What was he like?'

'A nasty piece, he were,' said my neighbour. 'He stood to inherit from old Emily. She used to tease him, she did. She'd say to him "that clock and this house don't like you nevvy, and no mistake. It won't chime if the house don't care for you. That clock won't chime after I've gone until the right person moves in here." '

I felt a peculiar sensation along my spine. 'And did he inherit?' I asked, keeping my voice level.

'Oh yes. Old Emily died and he moved in. He got the clock, too, along of all her stuff. But he couldn't get it to go for him, no matter how hard he tried. In the end I saw him come outside here and smash the clock on the slabs. Fair seething he was. Then he kicked it round the yard and buried the pieces.' My neighbour chuckled at the memory. 'He died not long after,' he continued. There was a note of satisfaction in his voice. 'Heart it was. Died clutching the mantelpiece where the clock used to stand.'

'Too much information,' I said, shivering.

'Ah, you've no cause to worry, lass,' he said with a wink. 'House likes you, no doubt. Fact was, no-one settled here for long. Some said they felt a strangeness, some said they heard odd noises.'

'Like the clock?' I interrupted. 'The clock chiming?'

He gave me a long, shrewd look. 'No not the clock as I ever heard. Just knocks and bangs, that sort of thing.'

I turned to look at the house. The evening sun shone into the tiny window panes, making them glow and twinkle. I frowned, lost in thought. 'I heard the clock,' I said slowly. 'I heard the clock chime. Miss Minton's clock.'

'Well lass,' he said equally slowly. 'I reckon old Emily has made you welcome. You must be the right person for the house at last…'